'Long live the Ki... ...think not, *agapi mou...*'

A sensation like a blow to the head made Penny's thoughts spin sickeningly, the room blurring before her eyes as she struggled to turn and look. To make her gaze focus on the dark, powerful shape of the man in the door.

It couldn't be. It just couldn't be! There was no way this was possible. It had to be a dream— or a nightmare—or both at once. Because there was no way it could be happening…

'Because to make that follow then, as you say, the first King must actually be dead…'

And, fixing his eyes on her shocked face, his burning gaze seeming to draw out all the blood Penny could feel had drained from her face so fast she thought it must leave her looking like a ghost, the new arrival took a couple of steps forward, moving further into the room.

'And as you can see, *gineka mou*, I am very much alive.'

'I— You—'

THE GREEK TYCOONS

Legends are made of men like these!

Modern™ Romance is proud to introduce you to…
the all new Greek tycoons

Modern-day magnates,
as gorgeous and god-like
as their mythological ancestors,
they put the 'man' into Romance!

This month:

THE GOOD GREEK WIFE?
by Kate Walker

*How will Penny cope
when her proud husband makes his return?*

THE GOOD GREEK WIFE?

BY
KATE WALKER

MILLS & BOON

First published in Great Britain 2010
Harlequin Mills & Boon Limited,
Eton House, 18-24 Paradise Road, Richmond, Surrey TW9 1SR

© Kate Walker 2010

ISBN: 978 0 263 87820 2

Harlequin Mills & Boon policy is to use papers that are natural, renewable and recyclable products and made from wood grown in sustainable forests. The logging and manufacturing process conform to the legal environmental regulations of the country of origin.

Printed and bound in Spain
by Litografia Rosés, S.A., Barcelona

Kate Walker was born in Nottinghamshire, but as she grew up in Yorkshire she has always felt that her roots are there. She met her husband at university, and originally worked as a children's librarian, but after the birth of her son she returned to her old childhood love of writing. When she's not working, she divides her time between her family, their three cats, and her interests of embroidery, antiques, film and theatre, and, of course, reading.

You can visit Kate at www.kate-walker.com

CHAPTER ONE

THE setting sun only barely lit the winding path that Penny was following, making it impossible for her to walk fast, however much she wanted to.

No, the truth was that deep down inside she wanted to run. She wanted to get away from the villa as quickly as possible, to run as far and as fast as she could possibly manage. She wanted to run and run and never come back, to get away from the poisonous atmosphere in the house she had left behind. But the truth was that up until now any such action had been impossible.

And now?

Well, now she knew that she could leave—perhaps she ought to leave. But doing so would be to admit to herself that there really was no longer anything more to hope for. That her dream of love and a future was over, gone for good. Dead like her fantasies.

Dead like…

No, even now she still couldn't put Zarek's name, her husband's name, at the end of that sentence. If she did that then she was admitting that everyone else was right and she was the foolish one, the only one who had taken so long to let go.

To admit that she no longer had a husband. That the man she had adored and married was never coming home again.

Reaching the spot where the path petered out onto the shore, she kicked off her sandals and paced onto the pebbled beach. Out at sea, she could just make out the dark shape of a small rowing boat and the man who sat in it, broad shoulders hunched away from her, his head just a black silhouette against the sunset. He was wearing some sort of hat—a baseball cap pulled down low so there was no way she could decipher any of his features.

Even now the thought of someone on the water made her shudder inwardly. Out there, somewhere thousands of miles away, Zarek had lost his life. The depths of the ocean were his only grave. That was what she had had so much trouble coming to accept.

And she was going to have to accept one further, even more hateful truth. The fact that even when he had been alive Zarek had never truly loved her. Their marriage had been a lie, on Zarek's part at least. To him it had been purely a cold-blooded plan for an heir, never the love match she had believed it. So why was she still holding onto his memory when it was so obvious that he wasn't coming back?

Finding a smooth outcrop of rock just above the tiny horse-shoe shaped harbour, she plonked herself down on the make-shift seat and rested her elbows on her knees, supporting her chin in them as she stared out at the small craft bobbing on the restless waves. Sitting there, just staring out into the darkness, she let her unwilling memory go back over the scene she had just left behind.

'Penelope…'

The voice had come from behind her, just as she reached the front door of the villa and had her fingers on the handle, ready to turn it. It made her freeze into stillness, keeping her eyes directed away and fixed on the heavy wood in front of her.

'Are you going somewhere?'

There was no mistaking just whose voice it was. Only one woman had that cold, distant tone that made her sound as if she were speaking through a cloud of ice, freezing the words in the air as they came out.

And only one woman called her *Penelope* in quite that way. Using the full version of her name to make it sound like a criticism or a reproach when everyone else—her own family or everyone who liked her—only ever used the shortened form of Penny or even Pen.

Not her mother-in-law. Or, to be more correctly precise, her stepmother-in-law.

'I thought I'd go out for a walk.'

'At this time of the day?'

'It's cooler in the evenings. And I prefer it that way.'

Still she didn't turn round. She didn't need to, of course, but more than that she didn't want to. She could already see Hermione Michaelis' elegant figure in her mind's eye. Slender to the point of emaciation, her hair kept unnaturally jet black with the constant use of hair dye, so that the few streaks of grey that were starting to appear were carefully disguised in an attempt to look so much younger than her fifty-nine years.

'I still haven't really adjusted to the heat in the daytime.'

'After so long?' her mother in law queried, making Penny bring her sharp teeth down on the softness of her bottom lip in an effort to bite back the instinctive retort that had almost formed on her tongue.

'So long' was only a relative term, depending on who used it. To Hermione maybe the past two years or so had seemed like an age. An age in which she had to live with her unwanted daughter-in-law, who now stood between Darius Michaelis' second wife and the full control of Odysseus Shipping, which was what she had been aiming for from the very first moment she had met Zarek's father.

And 'so long' barely described the past two years that Penny had lived through ever since the news about Zarek's fate had come through to the island. The news that had turned her life upside down, destroying the hope of future happiness, and taking away with it any chance of being able to tell her husband how she truly felt about him.

The brief time of her marriage seemed to have flashed by in the blink of an eye, but the two years since then had taken an eternity to live through. An eternity that had dragged out to seem longer and longer with every day of hope that perhaps this was the day he might return. And then the dreadful, appalling moments that had killed all hope of that for ever. Since then her life had been something to be endured, a desert to live through. Empty and arid, without the love she had once hoped for.

No, who was she kidding? Even before he had vanished— been killed, they said—Zarek had never offered her the love she dreamed of, Penny told herself with bitter realism. He had married her in a cold-blooded business arrangement, entering into a marriage of convenience because it suited him to do so, because he wanted an heir. And she was the one who had been fool enough to think it was something else.

'My skin is sensitive to the sun—and I don't want to burn. That can be so aging.'

The faint hiss of Hermione's breath in between clenched teeth told her that her deliberate dart had hit home. The older woman was paying the price for a lifetime of sun worshipping and the effects that none of her hugely expensive facials and even a recent facelift could really eradicate.

'So are you taking the dog?' Hermione turned the last two words into an expression of total distaste.

There was only one dog that she could mean. Argus, the great black and white hound who had once been so devoted to his master Zarek and who seemed to be the only other living soul who along with Penny mourned his loss. In the first few weeks after Zarek had gone missing, she had feared that they would lose Argus as well as the big sheepdog had pined for his owner, turning his head away from all food. But in the end he had transferred his devotion to Penny herself and now followed at her heel almost everywhere she went, lying under her desk when she had to work.

'I think not. He's already had a long walk today and the last time I looked he was fast asleep.'

Fast asleep on her bed if the truth was told but there was no way she was going to admit as much to Hermione. Her mother-in-law was only looking for an excuse to get rid of the big dog and Penny wasn't going to take any risks that way. Argus had kept her company when she had needed a friend most. His warm, reassuring bulk was there by her side in the darkness of the night. His long, shaggy fur had absorbed the tears she had shed on that dreadful night when the appalling truth that Zarek was in fact dead had been reported to them. The dog was the one living link to her lost husband and she would always love him for that.

'Nasty flea-bitten creature.'

Penny could practically see Hermione's mouth curl in disgust but she wasn't going to turn and check if she was right.

'There's one thing I can assure you and that is that my dog does *not* have fleas.'

Wrenching the handle roughly, she pulled the door open and stepped forward, enjoying the rush of air, scented with the tang of the sea, that flooded into her face. She felt trapped and confined—a feeling that was becoming the norm in a way that made her lungs constrict so that it was almost impossible to breathe naturally.

'Don't be long. It's getting dark already.'

Concern? Now that was new in a way that brought her head finally swinging round to meet Hermione's black glittering eyes. Immediately she knew that if she had been thinking that the older woman had her safety at heart, she was wrong. The light that was in that gaze was cold and predatory. The look of a cold-blooded buyer eyeing up her investment to check that all was well. Or a breeder with plans for producing a number of prize-winning offspring from a rather skittish brood mare.

No, that had been Zarek, Penny forced herself to acknowledge inwardly. He was the one who had seen her only as breeding stock for his dynasty.

'I'll be fine…'

'We need to talk to you…'

Penny's voice clashed with Hermione's, the sound of that 'we need to talk to you' making Penny's heart clench and thud roughly against the side of her ribs.

She knew only too well just what that 'need to talk' would entail. She had to. It was the one thing that Hermione and the rest of the family always wanted to talk about.

'I'll be back when I'm back,' she flung in defiance, pushing herself out of the door and into the freedom of the garden before Hermione could do anything to prevent her.

She almost ran down the path, her feet flying over the pebbles as they carried her as quickly as possible. She actually feared that Hermione would come after her, grab at her arm and drag her back, hauling her back inside the house to face 'the family' and the things they wanted to talk about. The older woman was capable of it.

Out at sea, the man in the small boat had given up on the fishing or whatever it was that had taken him onto the dark ocean this late. He was reaching for the oars, the powerful muscles in his arms and shoulders tensing under the white long-sleeved tee shirt as he began to pull against the waves. He must be a strong man, Penny reflected privately. Only someone with a great deal of muscular power could make that much progress against the swell of the tide. Watching him, she felt an unexpected shiver of awareness wash over her skin, perhaps as a result of the cooling breeze that blew in from the sea.

Or possibly it was the effects of the unhappy feelings that plagued her at the thought of that 'talk' that awaited her when she got back to the villa. When Hermione and her sons, Jason and Petros, would start on at her again, trying to persuade her to make the decisions they had been itching for her to come to for so long. At least they had had the sensitivity and the tact to let the last month go by without ever saying a word. They'd let her have the second anniversary of Zarek's disappearance, the day that marked the announcement of his death, without their insistent demands that it was time to look ahead instead of back, to plan the future, to 'move on'.

'Oh, Zarek…'

Dropping her face into her hands, Penny pressed her fingers hard against her closed eyes. Sometimes the misery could still grab her by the throat and make her wonder how she could live the rest of her life without ever seeing him again. He might not have loved her but she had adored him.

'I'll never forget you…'

But the realisation of the truth made the words catch in her throat even as she whispered them behind her hands. Because the truth was that with each day that passed she was finding it harder and harder to recall exactly the devastating attraction of her husband's forceful appearance, the powerful bone structure and sexual appeal of his stunning features. If she tried to visualise him against the darkness of her closed lids she found that the image danced and blurred before her and she could no longer form that once-beloved face in her mind.

The banging of heavy wood against wood jolted her out of her reveries. The fisherman had reached the land, his boat thudding against the pillars of the small jetty as he came up close. As she lifted her head to watch she saw him reach out to pull the vessel even nearer, his oars taken from their locks and dropped at his feet.

He really was a big man, Penny told herself, watching as the lean, powerful frame was silhouetted against the last of the sun, now sinking finally beyond the horizon. Tall, but not bulky—his rangy figure had a controlled power about it as he vaulted easily onto the jetty, bringing with him a coil of wet rope, the drops of seawater that fell from it glistening in the lingering remains of the light. It was the first time in so very long that she had even been aware of a man and how his body looked that she felt her heart kick hard against her ribs in a sense of shock at what she was thinking.

This much closer, she should have been able to see his face but the baseball cap that was pulled down low over his forehead hid so much. And the little that was left was concealed by the thick growth of a dark and bushy beard, which together with the overlong black hair falling onto the straight, strong shoulders gave him a wild, rather primitive look that made her toes curl into the pebbles in slightly shocked response.

Perhaps it was time that she made him aware of her. Let him know she was here.

'Good evening…'

No response. Clearing her throat carefully, she tried her amateurish Greek.

'*Kalispera.*'

That brought his head swinging round in her direction. She caught the flash of dark eyes narrowed against the setting sun and he adjusted his hat, tugging it down even lower as a defence against the glare.

'*Kalispera.*'

His voice was rough and unexpectedly non-friendly. Not aggressive; not hostile. Just very clearly not welcoming her approach. Which was unexpected and unusual. In all her time on the island never once had she approached the small town of Kioni without being greeted with warmth and friendliness from the locals so that her stumbling attempts at the Greek language had been no barrier at all to communication.

'Is the fishing good?'

What had she said now to make him stare at her for a moment so searchingly and intently that she felt almost as if his hidden gaze were a laser directed straight at her, threatening to shrivel her where she stood? Suddenly apprehensive, she found she was tensing, nerving herself for some sort of attack—not knowing what or why. Too late she wished that she had bothered to take the time to go and collect Argus and take him out with her on this evening walk. Not for nothing had the big dog been given a name that meant vigilant guardian, and if he had been with her then this disturbingly cold and unapproachable male would very definitely know to stand back, keep his distance.

Not that he showed any sign of actually wanting to approach her, because having considered her question for an inordinately long amount of time he suddenly shook his head abruptly.

'No,' he growled, tossing the word at her like a discarded piece of litter. 'Not good.'

And, turning away from her, he tugged hard on the rope to draw it up onto the jetty before looping it through an iron ring nailed into the wood and pulling it tight to fasten the boat to its mooring. A moment later he was crouching down to check that the knot was secure, the movement making the long, strong muscles in his legs and thighs bunch and flex as they took his weight

Again that disturbing shiver of response that Penny now knew had nothing to do with the cool of the evening in spite of the chill from the wind off the sea crept over her skin.

What was happening to her? Penny's head seemed to swim under the impact of the unexpected sensations, the unwanted thoughts that assailed her.

Was it really possible that the senses she had thought had died with Zarek were now coming awake again? Was she, as everyone had told her she would, finally really starting to take an interest in life again—in other men? But why would this man, this scruffy bearded, rough-voiced fisherman pique her interest so much? Or was it just that tonight she felt so lost, so alone that any man would act as a distraction from the bleakness of her thoughts?

Feeling uncomfortable and restless, she pushed herself to her feet but then found that she couldn't move, couldn't get away. Instead her gaze stayed locked on the strong, lean form of the man before her. Her throat felt dry and tight too, her heart thudding disturbingly so that she found it hard to breathe.

She should never have come out like this. Her tense mood and the uncomfortable meeting she had had with Hermione, the 'talk' she knew was coming, had all combined to knock her off balance so badly that she was no longer able to think straight. In fact she wasn't thinking at all, sitting here in the gathering dusk, her gaze hooked and held by a complete stranger. Yes, he had a good body—a great body—but was that enough to scramble her brain this way?

But then the fisherman stood up again and some movement of his head brought the little of it that was not concealed under the hat or the growth of beard into the light of a lamp at the side of the harbour. The sight of the jagged line of an ugly scar had Penny's breath hissing in sharply between her teeth, a faint sound of shock and horror escaping her involuntarily. White against the tanned darkness of his skin, it marred the line of dark beard on the right side of his face, skimming his temple and disappearing into the shadows thrown by his cap.

'Oh, my…'

The shocked exclamation died on her lips as something in her voice brought him swinging round to face her again. And everything about his stance, the way he held himself, the tension in the long straight spine and the way his hand clenched over the end of the rope that he held warned her that he had heard her response and that for some reason he didn't like it.

'That—that must have hurt…' she managed, her own body tensing warily under the burn of his dark-eyed glare.

'It did.'

His tone made it plain that he begrudged her the answer.

'And n-now?'

'*Ohi.*'

A shake of his head emphasised the denial.

'So how—?'

Hastily Penny caught herself up. What was she doing? Had she actually been about to ask him what had happened, how he had come by the injury? She must be crazy. Here she was alone in the darkness with a dark, powerful and clearly unwelcoming stranger and she was pushing him for answers he clearly did not want to give.

And why, why, was she even remotely interested? What was it about this stranger that had so unsettled her that she had actually wanted to know what had caused the injury that had marked him so badly? Wasn't the fact that it was so evidently the result of some terrible violence enough to clamp her foolish mouth shut?

'So many questions,' the fisherman mocked now, and the low voice carried over the silence to where she sat on her rock, some dark edge in it making her spine tense, her stomach twisting in sharp apprehension. 'Why so curious?'

'I…'

She was halfway to her feet, but the need to keep her eyes on the big, bulky figure silhouetted against the setting sun meant that she didn't dare to move too fast or too obviously for fear that she would show him how keen she was to get away.

'You…?' he queried, that disturbing note in his voice deepening worryingly. And he took a step forward, towards her. Pushing her to her feet in a rush.

'Penelope?'

Another voice broke in on them, coming out of the darkness along the shoreline. A male voice; a voice she knew and recognised.

'Penny?'

'Jason!'

She would actually have welcomed the arrival of any member of those she privately labelled The Family at this stage of things. But Jason was the only one of Zarek's stepbrothers who was actually kind to her. Closer to Penny in age than any of the rest of the family, and startlingly handsome—conventionally good-looking where Zarek had been dark and devastating—he had been approachable, even warm and sympathetic from the moment she had arrived on Ithaca as a young, naïve bride.

And it had been Jason who had warned her that Zarek's marriage plans had been the cold-blooded hunt for a wife who would give him an heir. A fact that Zarek himself had confirmed when she'd challenged him, asking why he'd proposed to her.

'Isn't it obvious? I couldn't keep my hands off you,' her husband had said. 'And I knew we would make beautiful babies together—and that's all that mattered.'

'You OK, *agapiti mou*?'

The term of affection was new, but it was what she needed. It was enough to have her on her feet and swinging round to him, nervous steps taking her towards him in a rush that had her almost tripping over herself on the slipping sand. Like a bird winging home to its nest, she ran straight for Jason, unthinking, hands reaching out to him.

Jason opened his arms too so that she ran into them, almost collapsing up against his hard length and burying her face in the crisp cotton of his shirt. Long arms came round her, holding her tight.

And that was when second and then third thoughts forced themselves into Penny's whirling brain, taking the instinctive, mindless fear that had pushed her into movement and pushing it aside, replacing it with a sudden feeling of having made a terrible mistake. Fear of the stranger was one thing, but from Jason's reaction he had taken her response to mean much more than she had meant. He was holding her too tight, too close.

Too close for what she really wanted.

'Penny…'

And that tone had altered, putting something new into the use of her name, a thickness she had never heard and certainly wasn't meaning to encourage. The fisherman might have spooked her, twisting her nerves into fearful response, but a sudden slow crawl of unease down her spine gave her the unwanted sense of out of the frying pan and into the fire.

'Jason…' she tried experimentally, aiming to lift her head from where it was pressed against his chest, ease herself away from the limpet grip he had on her.

As she had feared his arms tightened round her, holding her still. Already unsettled by her encounter with the fisherman, and painfully aware of the fact that he must still be watching her, she felt as if her head was about to explode with stress. She didn't want this and if Jason thought he had found the perfect time to make a move…

Suddenly she knew she had had enough. Enough of this situation, this family. She didn't belong here and she never had. She had always been second best, unwanted and unpopular with Zarek's stepmother and stepbrothers. And second best to Zarek too.

So why was she so determined to stay here where she wasn't wanted? To cling onto memories that had never really been true, no matter how much she might wish they had. Perhaps if she escaped, she could leave, go home. She could be by herself and try to find another way of living. She could always take Zarek with her in her heart.

And that gave her the perfect way to distract Jason, to turn his thoughts onto other, more important things—more important to Jason, anyway. Even if Hermione's aggression was not Jason's way, he was every bit as hungry for control of Odysseus Shipping as his mother.

'I want to call a board meeting for tomorrow,' she said, raising her voice so that she could be heard over the crash of the waves.

It worked. She felt the change as soon as she spoke, the new and different tension in Jason's body, the gleam in his eye that he couldn't disguise as he looked down at her. He even loosened his hold on her so that she could step back away from him.

'Why?' he asked, not sounding at all as if he believed there was any reason other than the one she knew he was hoping for.

'I'm sick and tired of this whole business, Jason.'

The tension that had gripped her earlier pushed the words out in a rush, giving them far more emphasis than she had planned.

'I want to get away from here, start living again. I'm tired of treading water. It's more than time this whole business was sorted out and everything finalised so that we can get on with our lives. I can't inherit unless we have Zarek's death declared and legalised. So let's do that. Let's put it all behind us—'

'I'll get onto it right away,' Jason broke in on her, his tone revealing only too clearly how much her words had pleased him. He even gave her another hug but thankfully it had lost the sexual overtones of the earlier one. His ambition and greed were a more powerful force—or perhaps, more likely, the sexual flirtation had only been used with the hope of bringing things to this point. Another reason to be glad that she had made her decision.

'Exactly how do you want to play this?'

But Penny had had enough. Painfully aware of their silent watcher, the unsettling atmosphere he had created, she just wanted to get back inside, seek the privacy of her room.

'Not now, Jason. Not here. He—'

'Who?' Jason questioned sharply. 'Who's "he"?'

'That man…'

Flinging out her arm, Penny gestured wildly in the direction of the harbour and the spot where the fishing boat was tied up.

'What man?'

'He…'

But Penny's voice died away as she turned in the direction

she'd indicated and saw only the boat bobbing at its mooring, the water lapping against the harbour side and the lamp illuminating an empty and silent space where the mysterious man had once been. He had gone silently and secretly, and she had no idea just what he had heard or seen or why it should bother her that he had overheard any of their conversation. But all the same, something uncomfortable and uneasy nagged at her mind at the thought that he had been there at all, and the rapid, uneven beat of her heart was the lingering effect of her unnerving and unsettling encounter with him.

CHAPTER TWO

HE WOULD need to be more careful in the future, the fisherman told himself as he headed away from the harbour and towards the small, single-storey, white-painted house that he had made his home since he had arrived on the island a few days before.

He had almost given himself away there, speaking English—speaking at all when it was so possible that Penny might recognise his voice and know that he was alive. Alive and back on Ithaca for the first time in over two years.

And he didn't want her to know that. Not yet. Not until he had had a chance to check the lie of the land, see just how things were. It might only have been two years—just twenty-four short months—since he had been on Ithaca, and a much shorter space of time since he had realised that the place even existed, but to him it felt so much longer than that. It seemed as if it were a whole lifetime since he had set foot on the island. Then he had thought that he would be back within the week. He had never anticipated that it would be years before he saw his home and his wife again.

But now he was back. And not before time it seemed, he told himself as the door to the cottage slammed shut behind him and he marched into the single, cramped living room. It

appeared that the reports he had been hearing were true. His
stepmother and her family were moving in on the business.
Hermione had always had her eyes set on Odysseus Shipping
and now it seemed that his absence had given her the encouragement she needed to make a play for control. And he knew
just how that control would be won. Through one of
Hermione's sons.

And Penny had run straight into *Jason's* arms. She had
been planning having him declared dead with his detested
stepbrother. And the wild fire of fury that had flared inside
him at the sight had been a struggle to bring under control. It
was fierce, it was unthinking, it was irrational, but the sight
of the woman—the *wife*—he had come back to find enfolded
in the arms of the man he knew had been scheming his
downfall for all of his adult life had had him fighting with
himself not to react in anger. Unable to stay and watch, he had
turned on his heel and marched away before the urge to
declare himself there and then had got the better of him.

Shaking his head, he fixed his eyes on the now moonlit sea
as it lapped against the edge of the beach below the cottage,
the slow, dark swirl of the waves suiting his mood completely.

Jason had already taken the first steps towards acquiring
what he and his mother had always wanted. His elder stepbrother had barely waited for Zarek's disappearance to be confirmed before he had been trying to apply for power of
attorney to run Odysseus Shipping. He hadn't hesitated to
make his move as soon as the opportunity had presented itself.
But of course the legal control rested with Zarek's wife.

With Penny, who had had a far greater return on her investment of time in their marriage than she could ever have hoped
to achieve.

Or thought she had.

He rubbed at the ugly scar that marked his temple, grimacing as the wound throbbed with the ache of memory.

That was one of the reasons he had come back to Ithaca in total anonymity, his true appearance obscured behind the wild growth of beard and hair. And it seemed that it had worked. Tonight he had come face to face with his wife for the first time in years and she had shown no sign of recognising him.

But just hearing her voice again had brought it all back.

'Go, then!'

The memory was so clear that he actually glanced up and in the mirror over the fireplace almost as if he expected to see that the door had opened while he had been absorbed in his thoughts and Penny had walked into the room.

'If you're going, then go! I don't know why you're even telling me this. It's not as if you're asking my permission!'

Shaking his head to try and drive the sound of his wife's voice, still shrill even after all these years, from his mind, he paced across the room to the window to stare out at the now moonlit sea where it lapped against the pebbles of Dexa beach. The wind was getting up, making the olive trees sway wildly in the breeze.

He was damn sure he hadn't been asking for permission or anything like it. The truth was that after the way their marriage had all but disintegrated in the short time they'd been together he'd firmly believed she would be as grateful for a break as he was. She'd even backed away from him sexually, and sex had been one of the things that had been right between them at the start. The glue that had kept them together.

'Just go—' she had flung at him, her sexy mouth distorting in the force of her rejection of him. 'But be warned, if you go, then don't expect me to be here waiting for you when you return.'

So had she waited? He'd thought she had when he had discovered that she was still here on Ithaca. He'd even allowed himself to wonder just for a moment whether she might hold out some hope that he would come back. From what she'd just said it seemed that it was the legalities resulting from his disappearance that had kept her here, not any lingering loyalty to her marriage.

But then she'd made it only too plain exactly why she'd married him in the first place. He'd been fool enough to believe her declaration that she wanted children—longed for them, she'd said—when in fact she'd been lying through her teeth. She'd even been taking the pill and when he'd confronted her with the evidence she'd thrown it back in his face.

'Bring children into this marriage—you have to be joking. Where did I sign up for that? Where was that written into the pre-nup you got me to sign?'

He'd never thought he'd need to do that. He'd signed and sealed the financial details, but never made them dependent on the one reason he'd determined on marriage in the first place.

And Penny had proved herself nothing but a scheming little gold-digger. She'd married him for those financial details and never intended to carry out her part of the agreement. Never intended to give him the heir he so longed for. Even if he had come back safe and sound from the *Troy*, she would still have come out of their brief marriage a millionaire in her own right. He had been happy to agree to very generous terms, never thinking he would have to fulfil them before he had even celebrated his first wedding anniversary. For ten short months of commitment, Penny would walk away with a huge profit.

But not as much as she would profit from his supposed death. From the will that he'd changed in her favour when they had married. One thing was clear. She wanted to realise her assets, get her hands on the company.

It must have felt like the answer to her prayers—as if all her birthdays had come at once—when he had done exactly what she'd wanted. He hadn't come back, leaving the field wide open to her. She hadn't even had to go to the trouble of divorcing him and so risking losing half the money she had married him for.

Pushing his hands through the long mane of hair, he faced his reflection in the mirror and saw the darkness in the eyes that stared back at him, the tautness of the jaw line under the thick growth of beard. Remembered anger tightened his lips until they almost disappeared. There was a way to deal with this that would have much more impact, and it seemed that Penny herself had just given him the perfect opportunity he had been looking for.

He'd been away too long—an absence he had not been able to do anything about—but the last week or two he had spent waiting and watching, just to see what he would be walking into when he made his return. That was all over now. The time for waiting and watching was past.

Heading into the tiny, primitive bathroom, he opened a cupboard and reached for scissors, a razor. It was time he came out from behind his concealing disguise and made his presence known.

Zarek Michaelis was back. And very soon the whole world would know it.

And so too would his errant, untrustworthy wife.

He was looking forward to seeing the look on her face when she realised that she was not going to get her greedy fingers on the fortune that she had hoped—believed—was hers. Or that the new life she had declared that she wanted would not be on the cards any time soon.

When she discovered that the husband she had believed

was dead and out of her life for good was in fact very much alive and ready to take back the reins of his previous existence.

'Penelope, it really is time to make a decision.'

Hermione leaned forward as she spoke, dark eyes boring into the face of the woman opposite her, long fingernails tapping on the polished wood of the boardroom table to emphasise the point she was making.

'We can't let things go on any longer as they are.'

'We?' Penny questioned, determined not to let Zarek's stepmother run this meeting, have things all her own way.

There was no escaping the decision that she had known she had to face some time. The decision everyone had been demanding she make for a year or more now. And deep down she knew she'd already made it. But it didn't mean that she was happy about it.

'We are all shareholders,' her mother-in-law pointed out, the bite of acid on the words making Penny flinch inwardly.

'Minority shareholders,' she flashed back, determined not to show how her stomach was tying itself in knots; the fight she was having to keep at least some degree of composure in the face of the bitterness of the inevitable.

'But nevertheless Odysseus Shipping is a family concern.'

It was Petros, Hermione's second son and Jason's younger brother who spoke, shifting his bulky form on his chair in a movement that echoed the impatience in his voice.

'And you are blocking us from playing a part in running the company,' he tossed over the table at her. 'We all need to put our expertise to work to keep it running—and growing. Without Zarek it has become a rudderless ship.'

His stiff tone and totally focused expression gave no sign at all of even noticing the pun.

'It needs someone in charge.'

'*I* am in charge,' Penny declared, stiffening in her seat.

This was how it had been from the moment that Zarek had first been declared missing. The rest of the family had barely given her time to register the loss of her husband, let alone grieve for him, before they had been putting pressure on her to find a new head of the family firm, and at least once every month they had dragged the subject of his successor up again. She'd tried to hold it together, she really had. But she'd had enough.

'It's a shipping empire,' Petros dismissed her protest with a contemptuous wave of his hand. 'A man should be in charge because we all know Zarek isn't coming home. And until things are made official then the company will always be in a shaky state. A prey for rumour and scandal in the papers. An insecure bet for investors.'

'You know what has to be done.' Jason leaned forward now to distract her attention. Obviously he had seen the way her jaw had tightened, her breath hissing in between clenched teeth, and he was clearly worried that she was going to go back on what she'd told him last night. 'Penny, it's over two years since Zarek went missing. There has been no sign of him, no word in all that time. It's time we accepted what we all know as the truth and had him officially declared dead.'

There. It was out. The words seemed to land on the table with a deafening thud, lying there in front of her in an almost solid form. Too real to reject or deny. But now when it came to it she didn't know if she could go through with this.

'It takes seven years to have someone who's missing officially declared dead.'

'Not in a case like this,' Jason reminded her. 'Not when there is so much evidence as to what really happened and that you can file a petition to have him legally declared dead. You know that everything points to the assumption that Zarek died that day on the boat. Even the pirate chief himself said…'

'I know what he said!' Penny's tone was sharp as much from the knowledge that she really didn't have a leg to stand on as from the fear of hearing those words spoken aloud again.

'That's him,' the leader of the pirates who had boarded the *Troy*, the boat that Zarek had been on on the very last day he had been seen, had said when they had shown him a photograph of Zarek during the investigation into what had happened. 'That's the one. And, yes, he's dead. I put a bullet in his head myself.'

He had been so openly defiant, so proud at the thought that he had killed one of the hated Westerners, the rich who had so much more than he and his band had ever had, that he hadn't even cared that he had convicted himself of murder with his own words.

'And then I watched him fall overboard into the ocean… He's shark food by now for sure.'

Penny shivered in spite of the sun beating through the window at her back. She had had nightmares about those words for months, could still wake up in a cold sweat with them pounding at her head, making her heart race in panic. In her nightmares she had seen Zarek's face as he had walked away from her, his expression cold and hard, eyes dark and shuttered. The knowledge that she had lashed out in her own pain, using the words that were guaranteed to drive him from her, still haunted her with the thought that they had been the last words he had heard from her. And now, when she saw him again, in her dreams, she knew that the glaze on his eyes was put there not by anger but something far more devastating.

'Then you know that the lawyers told us that someone who had been exposed to "imminent peril" like that and

failed to return can be declared dead well before the legal
time limit is up.'

'I know…'

She knew but she didn't want to face it. Making that
decision would mean admitting that Hermione and her sons
had finally dragged her down.

Suddenly in the distance there was a faint scream and a
crash that brought her head swinging round, eyes going to the
door from behind which the sound had come.

'What…?'

'One of the stupid maids being clumsy, I suspect,' Jason
commented dryly, shrugging off the interruption. 'I suspect
that means that our coffees will now be delayed. Penny…'

'And the girl will have to replace the broken crockery out
of her wages,' Hermione added snappishly, frustration at the
fact that things were not going her way obviously showing
in her voice.

Pushing back her chair, she got to her feet and headed for
the door, obviously determined to reprimand the poor girl
severely at the very least. And it was that small action that
pushed Penny out of her inertia, reminding her forcefully of
just why she had made her decision last night. Why she so
wanted to get out of here.

'You're so right, Jason,' she declared with force. 'Zarek's
gone and Odysseus Shipping is all mine to do with as I please.
So once the formalities are over—if we can work out terms—
then the company is yours, Jason.'

And she would be free to live her own life.

Reaching for the glass of water in front of her, she lifted
it, tilting it in Jason's direction in mockery of a toast, not
daring to lift it to her lips for fear that her throat had closed
up so badly that the water would choke her.

'The king is dead,' she proclaimed, making her voice sound as light and careless as she possibly could. 'Long live the king.'

Her words fell into a strange and disturbing silence. A silence that seemed to reach out and enclose her, tangling round her throat and making it impossible to breathe.

Suddenly Jason wasn't looking at her. He had turned away and was staring in the opposite direction. They were all staring that way. Everyone in the room had their eyes fixed on where the door had swung open, pushed firmly but not violently from the other side so that it created a wide, wide space. And everyone was staring into that wide space, shocked, stunned, almost as if they had seen a ghost. Even Hermione had come to a complete halt, one long, elegantly manicured hand going up to her throat in a gesture of horror.

'Jason…' Penny began, but the name died on her tongue, shrivelled on it by the realisation of just what was happening in the same moment that a voice—an impossibly, unbelievably, shockingly familiar voice—spoke, cutting across her in a rough, sardonic drawl.

'Long live the king? I think not, *agapi mou*…'

A sensation like a blow to the head made Penny's thoughts spin sickeningly, the room blurring before her eyes as she struggled to turn and look too. To make her gaze focus on the dark, powerful shape of the man in the door.

It couldn't be. It just couldn't be! There was no way this was possible. It had to be a dream—or a nightmare—or both at once. Because there was no way it could be happening that…

'Because to make that follow, then, as you say, the first king must actually be dead…'

And fixing his eyes on her shocked face, his burning gaze seeming to be drawing out all the blood that Penny could feel had drained from her face so fast that she thought it must leave her looking like a ghost, the new arrival took a couple of steps forward, moving further into the room.

'And as you can see, *gineka mou*, I am very much alive.'

'I—you—'

Penny tried to get to her feet but abandoned the attempt after only a moment, finding that her legs were too weak to support her. Her feet seemed to be balanced on a floor that was strangely uneven, rocking and swaying beneath her as if a huge flood had suddenly come along and lifted the house from its foundations, carrying it out onto the wildest swirling sea. And the look Zarek turned on her was cold and dark, one that killed any impulse to fly into his arms, even after the distance of these two dreadful years. It was a silent, black reminder of the fact that the last time they had been together they had ripped the fragile camouflage covering off their marriage and exposed the lies and deceit that were at the centre of it. Exposing it for the lie it was.

Slumping back into her seat, she shook her head faintly, sending her hair flying out around her face, then passed a shaking hand in front of her eyes, rubbing at them to clear them of this impossible hallucination.

But when she blinked hard and looked again he was still there. Dark and powerful and strong as ever with a forcefully carved face and deep burning eyes that seemed to flay off a much needed layer of skin, leaving her feeling painfully raw and vulnerable, totally exposed.

It had been so long since she had seen him in the flesh, rather than in the photographs she studied every day, that it was almost like seeing him for the first time. Seeing how devastatingly attractive he was, how big and powerful, his lean, rangy figure in the plain white shirt and steel-grey suit easily dominating the room and making everyone else look so very small and insignificant.

'Zarek …' she croaked, her throat closing up around the sound so that she could barely get it out. 'Y—you…'

'Indeed, *agapiti mou*…'

His response was a small, cynically mocking bow of acknowledgement, his probing gaze not leaving her face for an instant.

'Zarek Michaelis. Your absent husband. Home at last.'

CHAPTER THREE

HOME at last.

Who was he trying to kid? Zarek wondered. Even as he spoke the words he knew that there was no way this return felt at all like coming home.

Of course he was back on Ithaca, back inside the family house, the place where he had lived from his childhood and where he'd always looked forward to returning to whenever he'd been away. But somehow this time nothing felt the same. Nothing had that feeling of rightness, of completeness that it had had before.

Which was hardly surprising. After all, he had just walked in on a discussion of a plan to have him legally declared dead. With that on their minds, none of them was going to be glad to see him walk through the door large as life and infuriatingly, unfortunately alive.

Not even Penny.

Not even his wife, who had actually been toasting the fact that he was dead as he opened the door. And was now staring at him as if he was her nightmares come to life.

But what had he expected? That she would run to him on a cry of delight, fling herself into his arms? He'd be every kind of a fool if he'd even dreamed of that. She'd told him as much to his face. And last night would have taught him that dreams of her waiting for him were nothing to base his future on.

But forewarned was forearmed and so there was little to surprise him in the way that she just sat in her chair, slim and elegant in a dark green sleeveless linen dress, eyes wide, staring at him as if he had indeed risen from the dead right before her. If anything she seemed worse—even more appalled than Hermione, and his stepmother looked as if the devil incarnate had just risen up from hell to appear before her.

'So,' he drawled cynically, injecting dark mockery into his voice as the silence lengthened and dragged out. 'Is this any way to greet the prodigal son? I was expecting the fatted calf at least.'

'Then you should have let us know that you were coming!'

Hermione had managed to regain some control but the hiss of fury in her words betrayed the way she was feeling deep inside.

'Or even that you were alive—it would have been nice to know.'

'I did not know myself—that I was coming.'

Zarek couldn't be unaware of the way that his answer had only incensed her further, the flare of her nostrils, the flash of fury in her eyes revealing just what she thought of his response. But quite frankly he didn't give a damn. And he had no intention of launching into the lengthy and complicated explanation of how he came to be alive, and why he hadn't let them know about it until now. Not here and not in front of everyone including Odysseus Shipping's lawyer, their accountant and half the assembled members of the board, it seemed.

'I thought that I might wait awhile longer—and learn as much as I could about the home I was to return to. It has been an interesting experience to say the least. But suffice it to say that I am here. And I am staying. So…'

Leaning forward, he picked up a pen that was lying on the polished wood of the table together with a sheet of paper that held, as he knew it must, a precise order of business as prepared by Leander, whose obsessive concern for detail had not, it seemed, eased up any in the time he had been missing.

'So this…and this…'

With a rough slashing movement he scored the pen through the first point of business and then another and another. All of them dealing with the plans to have him declared dead and transfer the management of Odysseus Shipping to his stepbrothers, just as he had expected.

'…can go—and this…'

A couple more decisive strokes of the pen and the entire proceedings for the meeting had been obliterated apart from…

'"Any other business",' he quoted cynically. 'Well—is there any other business?'

One swift glance at the stupefied faces all around him gave him his answer and he screwed up the agenda into a tight ball and tossed it in the general direction of the waste-paper bin, heedless of whether it actually landed there or not.

'Then I now declare this meeting at an end. And you…'

His pointed look was directed at everyone not the immediate Michaelis family.

'Can go home.'

It was as if the command, and the general flurry of movement, with chairs pushed back and people getting to their feet, had broken the spell that had held almost everyone frozen in shock. Suddenly Jason—*Jason*—was coming towards him, his hand held out in greeting.

'It's good to have you back. Amazing.'

He actually sounded as if he meant it, Zarek reflected cynically, and if the grip that enclosed his hand was just a little too much, a degree over the top, then that was only to be expected. Jason had always been good at playing the brother card, the friendly smiling brother, when Zarek knew that deep down the younger man hated his guts for being the oldest son, the real son. The only one who would inherit.

Petros on the other hand, like his mother, could not conceal his displeasure and disappointment at the return of the man he must have hoped had gone out of his life for good, leaving the way open to a far wealthier future than he had ever dreamed of. He looked as if he couldn't get out of there fast enough and quite frankly Zarek would be glad to see him go. To see all of them go and leave him alone.

All of them except Penelope.

His wife was still sitting just where she had been when he had walked into the room. In that very first moment she had made a tiny movement, a sort of jump in her seat, and all colour had drained from her face as her eyes widened in shock. That was all.

And now she might as well be carved from marble, she sat so still and pale. It was impossible to read what was going on in her head, behind those clouded eyes. And it was almost impossible not to turn and walk out of the room, leaving all of them—but most of all leaving her—behind him.

Was that the face of an innocent woman? A woman who had been mourning the supposed death of her husband, living with his loss for the past two years? Or was it the face of a woman who, if the scene he had witnessed last night had anything to do with it, had been looking forward to moving on, taking with her the fortune she had earned through a few short months in his bed?

Where was the warm welcome that any husband had a right to expect under such circumstances? Where was the gasp of relief, the rush into his arms, the ardent embrace that told him how much he had been missed? That she was so glad that he was home safe. That she was so glad that he was alive and had come back to her.

But this was just what he should have expected from her on his return. Hadn't she threatened—promised—him that this was how it would be?

'If you go, then don't expect me to be here waiting for you when I get back!'

Once again Penny's angry voice, the furious words she had flung at him, echoed down through the years from the day he had left Ithaca and set out on the *Troy*.

'This marriage isn't worth staying for as it is. If you walk out that door then you are saying it's over…'

But he had walked out of the door. Of course he had. The trials for the *Troy* were important, vital if they were to get the new design completed and on the market. And he'd thought he was giving them both room to breathe, to think. But then he'd believed he'd be gone and back again in a couple of days. Not a couple of years.

So why was *she* still here? Why had she stayed? For him in the hope that he would come back and they could start again, try to do something to redeem the hell that their marriage had become? Or had the news of his 'death' reached the island soon enough to stop her from leaving as she had said she would? And what had she stayed for? The vast inheritance that would now be hers rather than the part-share that would have come to her in a divorce settlement? Or the closeness with Jason that perhaps had been there all the time, but he had been too blind to see?

The scar along his right temple throbbed and ached, making him rub at it in discomfort, and he caught the sudden twist of Penny's head in sharp reaction. So if she hadn't known who he was last night, she did now.

And it worried her, that much was clear from the look— of guilt?—of apprehension that flashed across her face.

'Welcome back…'

'Good to see you safe…'

The conventional greetings, the slightly tentative slaps on the back, a shake of his hand, were the instinctive responses of the men who had worked for him. But he barely really heard them, acknowledged them only in an abstracted way. His attention was focused solely on the woman at the opposite side of the room.

'And what about you, sweet wife?'

Zarek turned towards where Penny still sat at the far end of the table, an empty water glass gripped in a hand that was clenched rather too tight, with the knuckles of her fingers showing white.

'Wh—what about me?'

'Nothing to say?' he challenged.

'No…'

Nothing she could manage to get her thoughts under control enough to put into any sort of order, Penny told herself privately. Her head was still spinning, her mind totally unfocused. Now she knew exactly why the maid whose scream they had heard had reacted as she'd done, dropping the tray of coffee cups in shock at Zarek's unexpected and unbelievable appearance. In that first moment that he had walked through the door, Penny felt she might actually do the same and send the glass she held flying to the floor to shatter into a thousand tiny pieces, and it was only the polished surface of the table underneath it that saved it from destruction.

She had reacted on a violent sense of shock in the moment she had first seen him, half rising to her feet and then sinking back down again just as sharply, frozen in a whirling storm of complete disbelief, bewilderment and not knowing what to do. And just like the maid who had reacted so forcefully to Zarek's arrival home, she didn't know if she wanted to scream out loud in an ecstasy of joy or express a wild rush of fear at what she saw.

The first impulse—to get to her feet, dash towards him and fling herself straight into his arms—had barely formed when a sudden powerful blast of reality hit her in the face with the memory of how they had parted. The shock of it was what had had her staying in her seat when every yearning sense in her body wanted to drive her close to this man, to feel the warmth of his body, inhale the scent of his skin. She wanted to have his arms close around her, know their strength supporting her as they had done in the past.

But the terrible sense that she had no right to do that any more, not after what had happened, kept her fixed in her place. The fear that if she even tried then he would reject her with cold and hostile disdain weighted her down even more. She couldn't make herself move though her heart raced in confused excitement and her eyes were fixed in hungry yearning on the dark, lean—too lean, she noted in some distress—form of the man before her.

'There's nothing I want to say here.'

Because now it seemed as if just holding onto the tumbler was the only thing that was keeping her under control. As if the hard glass were some sort of lifeline that she was clinging onto in desperation and if she let go then the tidal wave of emotions that had been building up inside her all day would break loose and swamp her completely.

'I don't think we should discuss our private business in front of everyone.'

'No, you're right.' Zarek nodded unexpectedly. 'What we need to talk about is private and personal. We don't need to share.'

The last remark was made with pointed emphasis and an equally pointed flick of black, thickly lashed eyes in the direction of Jason and his mother and brother. The three members of the Michaelis family were lingering between Zarek and the door, clearly unsure as to what their next move should be. In public, before the other members of the meeting, they had needed to show a united front, to make it look as if they were delighted to see Zarek back and welcomed him unreservedly. That they were glad to have his hands back on the controls of Odysseus Shipping. But now, when everyone else had left, an uneasy calm descended on the room. An uneasiness that Zarek was aggravating by his comment about keeping things private.

'We all need to talk…'

It was Jason who put the words into the silence, the disquiet that Penny felt she could actually breathe in from the atmosphere.

'We need to know what happened…'

'And you will learn—in good time.'

Zarek spoke without taking his darkly burning gaze from Penny's face, the words almost tossed over his shoulder at his stepbrother. Jason was saying the things she should be saying. The words she couldn't find the strength or the courage to form on her tongue.

'But for now you will surely acknowledge that there are some things that are private between husband and wife and are not to be shared with anyone else?'

Was she deceiving herself, Penny wondered, or had that deep, slightly husky voice subtly emphasised that 'husband and wife' as if deliberately driving home the fact that here was something in which Jason's presence was not at all welcome? Staking a claim, so to speak, like some powerful wolf moving in to demonstrate possession of his mate, the wild hairs along his spine lifting in open challenge.

'Of course, but—'

'In good time,' Zarek repeated, reaching out a hand to the edge of the door and pulling it open wide, the meaning of his message clear. He wanted everyone out of here and Jason would be a fool to ignore the signs. They were dismissed and that was it.

But still he lingered, looking across at Penny, a question in his eyes.

'Penny?' he queried, appearing to check how she felt.

How *did* she feel? She supposed to some it would seem wonderful that her husband, this man who had been away missing for so long—who had once been believed to be dead—would lay claim to her like this. To them it might appear that he was still so ardently in love that he couldn't wait to be alone with his wife, to restore the links of their marriage, renew their relationship.

But recalling what had happened between them before he had left, the rifts that had opened up between them, dividing them from each other, she knew she couldn't see it that way at all. Oh, yes, Zarek wanted to be alone with her but for his own personal, darker reasons rather than any loving reunion. And she could only begin to guess at just what those reasons might actually be.

But, 'It's fine, Jason,' she said, exerting every ounce of control she could manage to keep her voice firm and even when inside her nerves were quailing at the thought of how far from fine everything was. 'Absolutely fine.'

Was there some light of approval in the flash of the dark eyes he turned in her direction? The niggling worry that there was also something else had her shifting in her seat, finding herself able to move at last. Her brain seemed to have started working again too, sending the message *Zarek is back*—Zarek is *back*!—into her thoughts in a mixture of wild delight and shuddering apprehension. What was she to think? Yes, Zarek was back—but just who was this man who had been missing for two years? And what had happened to him while he had been away?

Exactly who had come home to her?

CHAPTER FOUR

PENNY pushed herself to her feet as Jason, Hermione and Petros made their way out of the door, tight knots forming in her stomach at the thought of being alone with her husband for the first time in so long.

She had never felt like this before, not even in the very beginning when she had first known him and had become his bride so very soon after that. Then she had been fizzing with excitement, just waiting for everyone else to go and leave them alone so that she and Zarek could become truly man and wife.

She had been so sure then. Sure that he wanted her—that he loved her. After all, he'd married her, hadn't he? At barely twenty-two she had been so very young, so naïve in matters of the heart, and even more innocent of the force of physical desire. It was only later that bitter disillusionment had set in and she had come to realise that Zarek was more than capable of *wanting* without any sort of love.

The door was shut, everyone else was gone. Shifting from one foot to another, Penny nerved herself for whatever was to come. At least standing upright she felt better equipped to face him. She had always been considered too tall by most men, but never for Zarek Michaelis. Somewhere in his past family history there had been an ancestor—probably his Irish great-great-great-grandfather who was always referred to as The Giant—who had brought a gene for height into the family and Zarek had inherited that in maturity. Even at five feet ten, Penny had to tilt her head back slightly to meet his eyes.

'So now…' she said as he closed the door a little too firmly for her mental comfort. 'What…?'

But the words caught in her throat as if a knot had tied tight around them, preventing her from getting them out. She could only stand and stare as Zarek lifted a hand to the right side of his face, just by his temple, and rubbed at the skin as if something there was troubling him.

'Are you all right?' she questioned sharply. 'Is something wrong?'

When he didn't respond but simply stood, back stiff, shoulders tight, head turned away from her, she felt the rush of memory like a sort of stinging mental pins and needles flood into her mind.

Someone else had done just that. And not too long ago. The memory seemed to dance at the corners of her thoughts, slipping away whenever she tried to get a grip on it. But right now she had other, more important concerns on her mind.

'What is it? Zarek? Do you have a headache?'

Still he didn't answer but stood motionless as a statue so that she launched herself towards him, covering the short space between them in a matter of seconds and whirling round in front of him.

'Tell me what's wrong?'

Without pausing to think, she reacted instinctively, lifting her hand to cover his where it still lay against his face, pressing her fingers over his as she looked up into his dark, shuttered face, seeing the way his heavy lids had come down over the darkness of his eyes. Hiding them from her.

'Tell me!'

For the space of a couple of jerky heartbeats he didn't move a muscle, but then at last he shifted slightly, moving the weight of his body from one foot to another, and drew in his breath on a slow, deep sigh. The warmth of his flesh reached her through the fine cotton of his shirt and the movement brought a waft of a deeply sensual scent, the ozone from the sea, sunshine on skin, and underneath it all the warm, musky scent that was personal to Zarek alone.

And in a split second the mood of the moment had changed. Where there had been nerve-twisting apprehension there was suddenly a heart-stilling tension. In Penny's veins the blood seemed to pulse infinitely slowly, shockingly heavy. Her breath too seemed frozen, leaving her with her mouth slightly open, unable to inhale, unable to think.

All she was aware of was the feel of Zarek's skin under her fingers, the heat and the softness of it, with the power of muscle and bone beneath the supple flesh. It was as if sparks had flown from his skin to hers, holding her melded to him, unable to move.

And the burn along her nerves reminded her only too painfully of how it had once been between them. The way that she had never been able to resist his touch, his kiss. The way that her body was yearning for it, reaching towards him even now.

'Zarek…'

His name was just a whisper across lips that were suddenly parched and dry, her tongue seeming to tangle on the sound so that she had to swallow hard to ease the discomfort in her throat. 'Zarek…'

'No…' Zarek said, his eyes still closed against her, his voice rough and seeming slightly ragged at the edges. 'Don't…'

'Don't what?'

But then he opened his eyes and looked down into her face and she knew exactly what he meant. What exactly he did not want her to do.

He didn't want her to touch him. He was rejecting without words the feel of her hand on his, the connection of skin on skin. He didn't have to say a word; it was there in his face, in his eyes.

And that was when she realised just what a terrible mistake she had made. Impulse and concern had made her break through the barriers that she had felt between them. The barriers that she had erected in her mind in self-defence because of the need to protect herself from the shock of his sudden arrival, the memory of all that had been between them before he had left.

'So your wife is not allowed to touch you?'

'My wife… Were you ever truly my *wife*?'

His eyes burned into hers as he raised his other hand to fasten around her fingers, clasping them tightly under the warmth and roughness of his palm. And as he pulled at it, bringing it down and away from his face, the force of his hold made her wince as her fingers were squeezed together.

But a moment later the slight discomfort was forgotten as shock ricocheted through her thoughts, making her head spin.

'You!'

She spat the word at him as she fought for control, struggled with the need to lash out with the hand that was free or launch herself straight at him, pounding her fist on his chest.

'It was you!'

She had seen the long white line of the scar before but then it had gleamed in the cold burn of the moonlight, the only visible part of a face that had been hidden by a cap, the fall of long dark hair, a heavy beard. The last time she had seen that scar it had been on the face of the man she had believed was a fisherman.

'You were spying on me!'

The memories of the previous night, the recollection of Jason's arms around her, and the thought of those dark burning eyes watching her put a new tension into her voice.

'Spying?' Dark cynicism rang in Zarek's voice. 'That word implies that you have something to hide.'

'As opposed to you who was hiding from me.'

She shouldn't be doing this, Penny told herself. She shouldn't be taking the conversation down this route. What she should be doing was asking Zarek where he had been, what had happened to him. She should want to find out—she did want to find out—just how he had come by that dreadful scar and what had happened to him. But she couldn't make her mouth actually form the questions. Her tongue seemed to have frozen and her throat wouldn't work on those words. Instead she heard the provocative and aggressive words come out as a challenge.

The thought that he had come home earlier but had not let her know that he was alive burned in her heart. That he had hidden from her, watched her, waiting—for what?—for her to betray herself in some way, was like a knife twisting in the wound. She had once been convinced that when she knew that he was alive and well she would be so happy, and had even allowed herself to think they might just have a chance to start all over again.

And now this…

Did she need further proof that, whatever else had happened while he was away, nothing had changed his mind about their marriage? He still regarded her with suspicion, as someone who was not to be trusted. Not as the woman he had loved and missed. But then of course she had known that that was the case from the start.

'Don't you think that I had the right to find out just what had been happening while I was away?'

'You didn't want to see me? Ask me.'

Another of those darkly blazing looks told her that he didn't need to ask. That in his mind she was already tried and condemned without a chance of appeal.

'"I want to get away from here, start living again,"' he quoted cynically, leaving her in no doubt that he had heard every word of her talk with Jason. '"I'm tired of treading water."'

'You really shouldn't listen in to other people's conversations,' she flashed back, knowing with a sinking feeling in the pit of her stomach just how he would have interpreted it. 'Don't you know that it's a fact that eavesdroppers never hear good of themselves?'

'I'm sure that most never actually overhear their wife planning to have them declared dead.'

'You were dead! At least—I—we thought you were.'

'And that was how it suited you.'

His grip on her tightened as he spoke, crushing her fingers. But it was not the biting pressure that shocked her, rather the rush of wild electricity up her arm, tracking a burning pathway along her nerves that frightened her with its instant and shocking reaction. How could he still affect her in this way when deep inside she knew the truth about the coldness of his heart?

'I don't want this,' she managed, tensing her muscles against his hold, pulling herself away from him as far as she could while he still kept her hand prisoner.

She had to get away, to find some space and quiet in which to collect her thoughts and decide how to go forward.

'Let me go!'

If he reacted against her, if he held her tighter, pulled her close, then she did not know what she would do. The swirl of ambiguous feelings inside her head was like a tornado, throwing her off balance and leaving her unable to think.

'I said let me go!'

The speed with which he released her added to the sense of shock, making her sway and stumble, almost fall. But it was fear that he would come for her again that had her reeling away, grabbing out at a nearby chair for support.

'Don't come near me! I don't want you near me!'

Oh, you liar, you liar, her conscience reproached her bitterly. You weak, cowardly liar. She wanted nothing so much as his arms around her, his body close to hers, to hold her and comfort her, to warm her and melt away the hard core of ice that seemed to have formed at the centre of her heart.

But Zarek simply folded his arms across his broad chest and regarded her coldly through eyes that seemed to have been formed from burnished steel, polished so hard that they were opaque and closed off against her.

'Of course not,' he drawled with bitter cynicism. 'After all, you never really wanted me back.'

It was only what she'd told him. If you go, don't expect me to be waiting here when you come back. Bitter pain had made her lash out at the time, knowing she would rather die than have him realise just how much she had loved him when he had seen her only as a willing body to warm his bed—and a brood mare to conceive his child. But it still stung viciously to have her wild, unthinking words turned against her in this way.

'You've sprung this on me—appearing from the dead. I— need some time,' she managed, trying for appeasement but getting nowhere with it if the cold burn of his gaze was anything to go by. And the way those powerful arms were crossed tight over his chest was like a rigid shield, deflecting any appeal she might direct at him.

'Then take it.'

'What?'

With her own defences ready formed for battle, his sudden capitulation was so unexpected that it took all the defiance from her, leaving her limp as a deflated balloon.

'Take it.'

It was more of a command this time, snapped at her with contempt that was like a slap in the face. It seemed that he had had enough of baiting her, for now at least. That shocking, taunting mood seemed to have evaporated, leaving instead something that sounded disturbingly like a cynical weariness.

'If you need the time to adjust to the fact that the husband you hoped was dead—'

'Never *hoped*!'

She couldn't let that pass. No matter how terrible things had been between them, she had never once hoped he was no longer still alive. And she was appalled that he might even think so.

'How could I ever hope that?'

'Hoped was never coming back…' Zarek amended without even the tiniest amount of a concession in his tone. 'Then take that time. I know that I sprung my arrival on you and heaven knows I too need some space.'

It was like a slap in the face, making pain twist in her stomach. She felt as if the room were closing in on her, crushing the breath from her body, making her feel sick with distress. He had been back—what?—barely an hour, and already he wanted space—to escape from her.

'To accustom myself to being here again. It has been a long time.'

Something in his tone brought Penny up sharp, made her look at him more closely. Only now did she see the evidence of new lines about his nose and mouth, the tiniest flecks of grey in his hair at the temples. Evidence that hinted at the fact that his life hadn't been totally easy while he had been missing. She had forgotten everything that the counsellors had told them, the advice they had been given at the beginning of all this, when they had believed that Zarek might be found and might be on his way back to them before the end of the year.

Wherever he's been, they'd said, whatever has happened to him, he will need time and space to adjust. He was held hostage, his life was in danger. It was unlikely that he would be able to just walk into the house and take up his old life where he had left off.

The wave of reaction that swept over her at the thought made her feel sick and ashamed, a terrible sense of guilt pushing her into rash, unguarded words.

'I'm sorry—I should have thought—do you need anything—want anything? Have you eaten? A sandwich? Some coffee perhaps?'

She sounded like the most inexperienced and gauche hostess greeting a complete stranger for the very first time. And obviously Zarek thought so too from the way that his beautiful mouth twisted and his dark eyes gleamed with something dangerous and cruel. One long, tanned hand lifted in a flicking gesture of dismissal.

'No—nothing. If I need anything, I can find it for myself— or get one of the staff to see to it. I do still have the staff in the house, I take it?'

'Of course you do.'

Flinging the answer back at him, she emphasised the *you* so as to make sure he realised that she had heard and noted that arrogant '*I*', which made it plain that he was back here in his role as owner of the villa, MD of Odysseus Shipping, lord of all he surveyed.

And her husband.

And what of her then? As his wife did she still have a place in this house? And for how long? While Zarek had been missing she had had a role to play, but now that he was back...

Did he even still want her as his wife?

'Then you have nothing to worry about.'

And with that she was dismissed. As if she needed the message rammed home he turned his back on her, walking across the room to stare out of the window, one hand pushed deep into his trouser pocket, the other lifting once again to press against the scar above his eye.

In the doorway, Penny paused, half turned back to him.

'Zarek...'

But his only response was an impatient gesture of his dark head, repulsing without hesitation the tentative approach.

'Go!' he said and it was a command she would be a fool to ignore. 'Just go.'

Well, what had she expected? Penny asked herself as reluctantly she turned away again and made herself move away, letting the door fall shut behind her.

Zarek Michaelis. Your absent husband. Home at last.

The mocking words he had tossed at her sounded in her head as she walked down the long, sunlit hall, heading for the stairs.

He was home, but it was obvious that nothing had changed. And because of that the wonderful joy and delight she should have been able to find in his return were totally missing. Zarek was back in body perhaps, but in his mind, and most of all in his heart, he was as lost to her as ever.

Perhaps more so. Because at least the Zarek who had gone away had put on a good pretence of being her husband when they were together. He had made it plain that in one sense at least—the sexual one—he wanted her.

He had wanted her in his arms, in his bed. He had barely been able to keep his hands off her and at least that way she had been able to get close to him. Able to keep him with her.

But that had been before the dreadful row they had had; now it seemed that even that had waned, taking with it the only chance she had of holding him.

'Don't,' he had said when she'd touched him. And he'd kept his eyes closed to reinforce the rejection in his words.

Zarek had only ever wanted her sexually, never loving her. He had hidden it in the past, but it seemed that he was no longer taking the trouble to hide anything any more. His cold dismissal of her just now proved that. Even that wanting seemed to have died in the time he had been away.

She had got him back from the dead and finally lost him for ever all in the same moment, it seemed.

CHAPTER FIVE

THE sound of Argus scratching at the door and whining to be let out was what woke Penny from the deep, dark sleep into which she had tumbled, how long later she had no idea. Night had fallen while she had dozed and the room was now in almost complete darkness, with only the glimmer of the moon coming through the cloud-hazed sky to throw any light onto things.

'Argus—no!'

The words came automatically, the result of so many other mornings being woken like this, and feeling afraid that Hermione would hear and be outraged both at being woken so early and the damage she would declare the dog was doing to the door.

'Stop that! Give me a minute and I'll…'

The words faded as she came more fully awake, sitting up on the bed and looking around her, her thoughts blurring as the truth of reality hit home.

It wasn't morning, she realised, it was evening. Late evening on the day that her life as she knew it had been turned upside down.

Late evening on the day that Zarek had come back from the dead.

'Zarek!'

Just the thought of him had her almost leaping from the big double bed, whirling round to stare at the side of it where, during the days of their marriage, Zarek had always slept. This was after all his bedroom, so wouldn't it be logical that he would come in here if he wanted to sleep? She had been so deeply unconscious that he could have come into the room, into the bed, and she wouldn't have noticed. She couldn't begin to decide if the shiver that ran down her spine at the thought was one of excitement or dread. How would she have felt if she had woken to find her husband lying beside her in their marriage bed?

'No!'

Shaking her head to drive the tormenting thoughts away, she pushed herself into action, hurrying across the room to open the door and let Argus out. Freed, the dog hurried off down the corridor, claws pattering on the polished wooden floor. The whole upper part of the house was in total darkness and she had to grope her way along before she could find a switch to bring some light to the place.

'Argus—wait…'

She should have checked the time before she'd left the room. Her watch was still on the bedside cabinet and she felt so disorientated that she had no idea how late in the night exactly. The last thing she wanted was to disturb the household and have Hermione and her sons descend on her, full of complaints.

And Zarek?

Once again her nerves twisted so sharply that she almost missed her footing and went tumbling down the wide, curving staircase. She had no idea where her husband was or what he might have been doing while she had been asleep. And not even knowing how long—hours, or just minutes—she had been away from him, she couldn't even start to guess.

She had never intended to fall asleep. The only thing she had wanted was some time to herself, in peace and quiet, to try to adjust to what had happened and to bring herself to some sort of acceptance of the way that her life had been turned totally upside down in just a few short minutes. But the way that Zarek had dismissed her, ordering her from the room with that aggressive movement of his head, had shaken her to the core. She had sunk down onto the soft surface of the bed with a sigh, then flung herself back against the pillow and closed her eyes, meaning to force herself to try and think…

But the images that had floated across the screen of her eyelids had made any sort of rational thought impossible. All that she saw was a stream of snapshots of Zarek, the man she had adored, had loved to call her husband, in the days before the terrible realisation that she had never truly been the wife of his heart. Her mind had taken her back to their wedding day, not quite three years before, when she had walked down the aisle towards where he stood by the altar, tall and proud, devastatingly handsome—and totally secure in his own skin.

She hadn't been able to believe that this man had even noticed the insignificant junior secretary in the import and export business that worked so often with Odysseus Shipping, let alone asked her to marry him. And that he was here, now, prepared to go through with the ceremony. Only the previous night, for the first time since their engagement, he had let slip the cool, courteous mask that he wore when he was with her, and had finally revealed a burningly sensual, fiercely passionate man underneath.

That night had shown her that Zarek did at least want her with a desire that had stunned her. A heated hunger in which the words cold and rational had no place at all. And then she had been happy to give herself to him because she had believed she really was loved. It was only later, when she had come to know the truth, that she had started to withdraw from him.

Remembering it again now, Penny felt her legs tremble beneath her and she had to grab at the banisters for support. She'd fallen asleep on the memories of her wedding night and as a result her dreams had been filled with wild, erotic fantasies that had had her tossing and turning in the throes of burning need.

She hadn't felt like that since the first lonely time when Zarek had left for the test voyage for his yacht, the *Troy*, walking out on her in anger, to give her time to think, he had said, to get her head together. And then later, when he had been declared missing, and when she had believed he was never coming home. The yearning hunger, the aching need— the physical need, at least—had slowly subsided over the last year, but it seemed that all Zarek had to do was to walk into a room and once again she was swamped by a tidal wave of need, one that had hit her with its full strength in the moment that she had touched him, and that now had sent disturbing echoes through her dreams.

But Zarek had clearly not felt the same.

'*No,*' he had said. Just a single word. But there had been such total rejection in his tone, and in the coldly burning look that had accompanied it, that she could have been in no doubt that total rejection was what he meant. And rejection was all he felt. Even the burning passion that had once flared between them had gone now, dying as a result of whatever had happened in the years he had been away.

But would it have been any different if the hijack had never taken place? If he'd come back three days later as had been planned. Penny felt as if something cold and nasty had just slid down her spine at the thought. Zarek had married her because he wanted a child, an heir who would ensure that Odysseus Shipping stayed in the family and there was no risk that it would ever come under the control of his stepmother and brothers.

The ground floor of the villa was in total darkness too, still and silent as if everyone had left, abandoning the place. But going where?

And where was Zarek? Would he have actually left, so very soon after arriving home again? A cold hand seemed to squeeze at her heart at the thought that he might just walk out and never come back again. Simply leaving her with the knowledge that he was alive and so was their marriage. But a marriage that it seemed he did not want any more.

'Zarek?'

Uncertainty made her voice wobble as she called out into the darkness.

'Anyone there?'

A deep bark startled her, making her jump as Argus suddenly lifted his head and pointed his narrow black nose in the direction of the garden room. Another bark, shorter and sharper this time, before the dog took off at speed towards the scent or the sound that he had detected. Not for Argus the indecision and hesitation that came from not knowing what his reception would be. He was totally sure of his welcome and he bounded through the partly open door, his joy and excitement evident in every movement.

But then Argus had it exactly right, Penny reflected, following the big dog at a much slower pace. Zarek would of course be overjoyed to see him.

'Argus!'

The delight in Zarek's deep voice reinforced her belief that he would be more than happy to see his hound and prepared Penny for what she would see as she went into the room herself.

The moon was shining through the big patio doors that were open to the sight of the gleaming waves that swayed and tossed between the cliffs and the horizon, the sound of them breaking against the rocks on the shore. Zarek sat in a wide comfortable armchair just inside the room, his face, his whole body, in shadow.

'Argus!' he said again, slapping one hand against his thigh to call the dog to him. A moment later he was cradling the animal's big black and white head in both his palms, rubbing the rough fur and crooning softly in low-toned Greek. And Argus, instead of bounding round his master in overwhelming joy at his return, as she had expected, simply gave himself up to the bliss of being reunited. His eyes closed and the only thing that moved was his big tail that was wagging furiously.

It was foolish to be jealous of a dog, Penny told herself. But at the same time she couldn't help envying the hound's simple pleasure in the moment. And his total confidence that he would be welcome, that Zarek would be as delighted to see him as he was to see his master.

It would all have been so much easier if she could have run straight into her husband's arms in the moment that he had first walked into the room. But of course Argus had endured none of the distance, the arguments, the stand up fights that had marred the days before Zarek's departure. He was loved for what he was, not given house room simply because of what Zarek wanted from him. And, besides, he was happy to acknowledge the man as his master and to obey his every command.

Penny couldn't help feeling that if, like the dog, she had come when called, or at the slap of a hand against a thigh, then things might not be so tense and awkward. Instead they were like two opposing armies, facing a stand-off, waiting for the instruction either to attack or stand down. And she didn't know which one was most likely.

But how she longed to hear the gentleness in her husband's voice that he now directed towards the hound, or to feel his hands on her, stroking, caressing as they were moving over the animal's big head and down his long back.

'You kept the dog.' Zarek's voice broke into her uncomfortable thoughts, making her start slightly, lifting her eyes from the dog's black and white head to look into her husband's face. Not that she could see anything of Zarek's expression. The darkness of the shadows by the wall was too intense, hiding everything.

'Of course I kept him,' she managed stiffly. 'What else did you think I'd do?'

'He wasn't your pet. And you were never that much of a dog person.'

'No. But of course I kept him at the beginning when we still thought that you might come back.'

She wasn't yet going to admit that at the beginning the dog and his needs had seemed to be the only things that had kept her going. That the reason he slept on her bed was because she hadn't been able to sleep alone and that most nights she had wept into the dog's shaggy fur. Zarek might never have loved her but she had loved him and the thought that he was lost or dead had torn at her already wounded heart.

'Besides, he pined for you so I had to look after him—and after that Argus and I—came to an understanding.'

'Thank you for that.'

Zarek's strong fingers were still buried in the rough fur, Argus' head on his knee, the dog looking up into his master's face with such blind devotion that she felt tears sting at her eyes. Once she had felt like that, hungry for Zarek's attention, desperate for any casual word that fell from his lips, any caress he offered her. But that had been before she had realised that she was only ever second best and that the man she loved didn't feel the same way about her.

'It's very dark in here,' she said abruptly, needing to break the mood.

Swinging away, she searched for the light switch, found it. Her fingers were on it when Zarek spoke sharply from behind her.

'Don't!' It was a command not a request but a moment later he softened it slightly by adding, 'I always loved the sight of the moonlight on the waves. I missed it.'

This was her cue to ask where he'd been while he'd missed the sea, but even as she opened her mouth to do so her nerves failed her. She was manoeuvring in the dark, both physically and mentally, and she was having to grope her way slowly through the shadows, trying to find some sort of a path that would help her.

'Whatever you want.'

She moved to a chair opposite him. At least this way the light from the moon gave her some hope of being able to read the expressions on his face.

'What time is it?'

'Around eight.'

Zarek didn't even trouble to glance at his watch. It seemed that the hour was a matter of total indifference to him. He couldn't care less if it was night or day.

'So late?'

How had she come to sleep so long? Was it the exhaustion after the stress of the day? Or the rush of relief at knowing that Zarek was home. That he was safe. She still couldn't quite absorb the fact for all that she was sitting looking at him with the sound of his voice in her ears, the scent of his skin reaching her nostrils. Her fingers itched to reach out and touch, to reassure herself that he was real. To feel the warmth of his flesh under her hands. But the fear of how he might react held her back.

She didn't feel she could take another of those cold-eyed rejections. Not now with what seemed like several layers of her skin flayed away, leaving her nerves raw and exposed.

'Where is everyone?' she asked to distract herself.

Normally at this time the staff were busy preparing the evening meal. The family would meet for drinks before dinner. But of course there was no way that this was any sort of an ordinary day.

'Gone.'

'Gone where?'

Zarek's shrug dismissed the question as unimportant.

'Home—or wherever they spend their evenings.'

'Everyone?'

This time his only response was a curt nod.

'Even Jason—and Hermione?' Penny found it hard to believe that Hermione would relinquish her place in the family home after she had been so determined to move in.

'Even Jason—and especially Hermione.' Zarek didn't give either of the names any particular emphasis but all the same it seemed to Penny that they had a dark underlining to his tone.

'How did you persuade Hermione to leave?'

She hadn't been able to achieve that herself in almost two years, even when she had asked Zarek's stepmother point blank to go. Since then Hermione had been a constant, nagging presence, critical of everything she did.

'If she wanted to keep the generous allowance she receives

from Odysseus Shipping then there was no argument.' The cynicism that twisted Zarek's mouth sounded darkly in his voice. 'She was very easily persuaded.'

'So there's no one here?'

Was that slight shake in her voice apprehension, relief, or even a strange sort of anticipation? Penny couldn't begin to decide for herself and, from the faint frown that she saw draw Zarek's dark brows together so briefly, neither could he.

'No one but us—and Argus.'

Zarek moved at last, getting to his feet to open the big glass doors to the garden so that the dog could go outside. Once again Penny felt an affinity with the hound as he padded reluctantly forward, obviously needing to get outside, but wanting to be sure that Zarek would not disappear again if he turned his back. Did she look at him like that? she wondered. Could the sense of disbelief, the fear that it might all be an illusion after all, show in her eyes when she watched him?

'But why?'

'I thought we had a lot of catching up to do. We need to talk. And that we would do it better if we were on our own.'

'Oh.'

It was all she could manage, and the gulp as she swallowed down the word gave away more than she was at all comfortable with.

Zarek turned from the door, leaning back against the wall and pushing his hands deep into the pockets of his trousers. Penny knew it wasn't possible but he really did seem to have grown bigger in the last few moments—taller and stronger and darker. And definitely more dangerous, with that ominous 'we need to talk' sounding like a warning bell for what was coming next.

CHAPTER SIX

SHE WOULD HAVE LIKED to have got to her feet. At least then, standing up, she would have been more on a level with him. But she would also betray her discomfort, scrambling to her feet like a frightened child, and moving uncomfortably from one foot to another.

'Don't you think you should eat first?'

That at least would give her an excuse to get up from her chair. And if she could spend some time on practicalities like preparing food in the big kitchen then it would be a distraction from his threatening presence, the discomfort of being here like this with a man she knew so well in some ways and yet who was a total stranger in others.

'I'm not hungry.'

It was a dismissal of what he had recognised as her attempt at diversion, she knew. He had no intention of being dissuaded from the path he was determined to follow.

'Though I wouldn't mind a drink,' Zarek conceded.

'Of course…'

She was on her feet and turning towards the dresser where the wine was kept when the foolishness of her actions hit home. This was Zarek's home after all.

'No, I haven't forgotten,' Zarek murmured dryly seeing her

hesitation, the embarrassed look she turned on him. 'Two years is not so very long.'

'It seemed long enough!' Her temper flared again, setting her off balance once more. 'No sign of you, no word from you. I didn't know what had happened—'

'I was hardly in a position to give you a phone call,' Zarek cut across her, breaking into the flow of reproach like the slash of a knife. 'How did Hermione end up living here? Did you invite her to move in?'

'No, I did not! She invited herself and wouldn't take no for an answer. Have you ever tried to get your stepmother to do something she didn't want to do?'

'As a matter of fact I have.'

Zarek expertly removed the cork from a bottle of rich red wine and poured a generous amount into a couple of glasses.

'Well, I don't happen to have the promise of a generous income—or the threat of withholding one—to dangle over her head like a carrot. Hermione arrived when the news of your disappearance had just broken—I didn't know what to do for the best. I thought it might after all be an idea if we were all in one place until we found out just what had happened.'

And she had been reeling in shock and distress. It didn't matter how she and her husband had parted, learning that his yacht had been hijacked by pirates and Zarek himself taken hostage had left her unable to think straight, so that she hadn't had the strength to fight Hermione over anything.

'And Jason…'

Something in the way that Zarek reacted—or, rather, his complete lack of reaction—sent her a warning signal that she was entering dangerous territory. She knew what Zarek had seen and heard on the harbour front only the day before. Her husband might not love her but he was her husband and a traditionally possessive, jealous Greek husband at that. He would not take at all kindly to seeing his wife in the arms of another man. Particularly if that man was his hated stepbrother.

'And Jason…' Zarek prompted almost casually, holding out one of the glasses of wine towards her. Because of the darkness in the room, she couldn't read his face properly but the stiffness of his long spine, a clipped edge to his use of his stepbrother's name, made all the little hairs on the back of her neck lift in wary apprehension.

'Jason dealt with all the practical things—liaising with the police, the press. He was very—helpful.'

Besides, Jason had been kind and considerate then and his support had been welcome at a time when she most needed it.

'Good for Jason.'

It was impossible to interpret the strange note in Zarek's voice as he lifted his glass to his mouth and took a deliberate sip of the wine. But Penny didn't care what his mood was. If there was any doubt in his mind about what he had seen then it was time she made things perfectly clear. His opinion of her was low enough as it was. She didn't want to add any further complications to the already explosive mix.

'We're not lovers,' she said starkly and saw his head come up very slightly, though he controlled the movement almost at once.

'Did I say anything?'

'No—but you're thinking it.'

'Oh, is that what I'm thinking?'

Another slow deliberate sip of his wine, but, watching him, Penny saw how long it took him to swallow it. The burn of his eyes challenged her with the fact that he could have been thinking something else entirely but she wasn't yet ready to go there. Better to clear the air with the things she could deal with here and now rather than rake up old problems and risk ripping open old wounds.

That would have to come, but it was early days yet—not even days! She was still feeling her way with this man who was her husband and yet, after the time he had been missing, now seemed like a stranger to her. She knew his face, his stunning features, his voice, his mannerisms. But was the Zarek she had married, the Zarek she had been intimate with, made love with—no, no—the man she had had sex with—still inside this façade that was so well known and yet somehow totally unfamiliar to her? For now she would do better to stay on safer ground. If Zarek's detested brother could ever be considered safer.

'I know how it might have looked to you, but if you'd stayed around last night then you'd have seen how I pushed him away.'

'Forgive me—' the twist to Zarek's mouth, the cynical emphasis to the words made them anything other than a genuine apology '—but I was still trying to absorb the fact that my wife wanted me declared dead.'

'Not wanted. It was the only practical thing to do.'

'And of course you have been carefully planning the most practical way of dealing with things. With Jason's help.'

'I needed someone's help.'

Penny drank some of her own wine, feeling the rich red liquid burn its way down her throat. The kick of the alcohol entering her blood gave an added spark to the volatile cauldron of emotions bubbling inside her. Sick and tired of managing in the dark—in all ways—she ignored Zarek's previous command and moved to click on the nearest lamp, flooding the room with light before swinging round to face him with a challenge.

'And as you said, *you* were hardly in a position to do anything.'

She was not sure if the light was now helping or actually making matters worse. Yes, she could see Zarek's expression, but did she really want to know just how intent his eyes were on her face? Did she want to look into their dark depths and see the burn of suspicion, the coldness of contempt? And in the light her eyes were once more drawn to the ugly scar that marked his temple, twisting and distorting the beautiful bronzed skin.

Impulsively her free hand lifted again, needing to touch it, to touch him. She wanted to reassure herself that he truly was real, and at the same time she had a crazy, irrational need to smooth her fingers over that scar as if by doing so she could ease the long-ago pain the wound must have caused him.

But something that flared deep in those stunning eyes had her wrenching her hand down again, clenching it into a fist at her side. She took another swift, snatching drink of wine to bolster her courage.

'What did happen to you?' she asked brusquely, not having enough self-control to try and think of some more careful way of phrasing the question. 'We were told you were—dead.'

'You heard about the pirates?' Zarek asked, moving to the open patio doors where he leaned against the wall and looked out into the garden, watching Argus, who was happily investigating something that clearly smelled very appealing.

Penny nodded.

'I found it hard to believe at first. It doesn't sound at all twenty-first century. But since you were taken, there have been several other ships that have been boarded by pirates. We saw the reports on the television—saw the pirates get into that small boat and leave the yacht. But at the time we didn't know that you were with them—that they'd taken you hostage.'

'No one knew.'

Zarek sipped at his wine again, staring out into the moonlit garden, his attention, his focus, seeming to be totally elsewhere. In an absent-minded gesture he lifted his free hand and rubbed at the ugly scar on his temple, making her shiver in distress at the thought of how he had come by it. She hated to see the evidence of that hurt, was saddened by the way that it marred the male beauty of his face. But, at the same time, in some way it only added to rather than detracted from the powerful impact of his forceful features.

'The small boat they tried to get away in was covered so the troops who were going to board the ship couldn't see inside. It was pitch black in there—foul.'

With another swallow of his wine, Zarek frowned at the gleaming path the moonlight made along the sea.

'They were all nervous, panicking—possibly high on something…'

Penny found that the glass she held was shaking violently as her hand trembled in reaction to the stark, matter of fact way he was reporting the story. He might have been talking about someone else entirely—or recounting a story he had heard. She could only imagine with horror how it had felt to be in that situation. To be trapped in that small, dark boat, bobbing on the expanse of the ocean in the middle of the night, with a group of pirates who were all out of control and even more dangerous as a result.

And the last memory he would have had of her was of the angry, lying words, she had flung at him before he had left for the *Troy*.

'They were arguing amongst themselves. Some of them wanted to use me as a hostage—to try and get a ransom out of the company at least.'

With an effort Penny tried to raise her glass to her lips.

Perhaps a taste of wine might calm her nerves, reduce the sense of revulsion she felt at the thought of Zarek being trapped in that situation. But her hand was shaking even more, so that she couldn't manage it.

'And then when the shooting started all hell broke out.'

'Oh, my—'

Zarek's head swung round as Penny finally lost her grip on her feelings and slammed down her drink on the nearest window sill, crashing it against the window.

'Penny?'

'They said…'

Her throat closed over the words, refusing to let them out, and her eyes were wild as she looked into his dark gaze. Swallowing hard, she tried again.

'They said—he said—that he p-put—'

It was unbearable to think of the words, let alone say them. And even with Zarek standing there before her, whole and safe, making a lie of the pirate leader's claim, she still found the idea too horrific to contemplate.

'He said that he put a bullet in you—your head.'

Burning tears were swirling in her eyes, blurring her vision, but she recognised rather than saw the now-familiar gesture as he rubbed at the scar once more. And the thought of how he had come by it made her dig her teeth in hard to her lower lip to hold back the moan of distress that almost escaped her.

'Then he gave himself rather too much credit.' Zarek's voice seemed to come from a long way away. 'And exaggerated his success. He might have planned to do that but the truth is that he missed. His aim was off. The bullet grazed my head and knocked me flying—out of the boat and into the sea. Penny?'

His question was sharp, urgent, his tone changing completely. And suddenly he was right beside her, having moved up close, his powerful body almost touching hers as he stared down into her face. And when Penny ducked her head to dodge that searing, probing gaze, he dumped his wine glass down beside hers and put a strong warm hand under her chin, lifting her face towards his.

'What's this?'

It was impossible to resist his control as he turned her face to the left, into the light, and she could sense the frown that drew his dark straight brows sharply together.

'What's this?' he demanded again, his voice rougher now and his accent deepening on the hard-toned question. 'Tears?'

Penny fought to twist her chin away from his forceful hold, to hide her betraying expression. But finding she wasn't strong enough, instead she lifted a shaking hand to dash roughly at her eyes, brushing the moisture from her lashes.

'Yes, tears,' she flung at him furiously, determined to face it out now.

Of course he hadn't expected tears. They had never had that sort of a marriage—at least not in Zarek's mind. And the bitterness of that bit so deep that she was almost out of her head with the agony.

'And what's so shocking about that, hmm? What did you expect? Laughter? Three cheers?'

'You would have cared?' He actually sounded stunned.

'Of course I would have cared! And not just "cared" in the past but still care now! I might not want to be married to you any more, but I sure as hell would never, ever have wished you *dead*!'

The last word came out on a choking gasp. One that was as much from the sensual shock of realising just how close he was now as from the anguish that came with the memory of how it had been when she had really thought that he had died in the pirate attack.

'So you thought of me once or twice in the time I was away?'

'Yes, I thought of you! We might not have had a marriage worth saving but there were—things—about you that I—that I missed…'

Her throat dried in a sudden rush of heat as she foolishly looked up on those words and met the burning fire of his gaze. Her heart skipped a beat then lurched into a rapid, thudding rhythm that was almost painful as it slammed against the sides of her ribcage, sending the blood pounding through her veins, pulsing round her head.

How could something so dark blaze so fiercely? she wondered as she felt herself come close to melting in the intensity of his eyes. The effect was doubled, strengthened all the more because it met with exactly the same feeling inside her own body. The same hotly yearning hunger. The aching need that drove all rational thought from her mind and left just a burn of molten desire.

'Penny…' Zarek said slowly and his voice was ragged at the edges so that she knew the need that had her in its grip had taken hold of him too.

So what had happened to that cold command of 'Don't'? There was no rejection, no distance in the look he turned on her. It was pure fire and lightning, searing where it landed. And it landed on her hair, then on her eyes, then burned across her mouth so that she opened her lips in a gasp of much-needed air.

And then forgot to breathe at all as Zarek reached out his hand and touched her cheek. Still holding her eyes locked with his, he let his fingers trail down to the side of her jaw, following the line of the bone until his touch reached her still-open mouth. His thumb rested on the lower lip, pulling it down very slightly, very softly. And she couldn't resist the temptation to slide out her tongue to taste it, taking the essence of his skin into her mouth as she did so.

Which immediately made her want more. Her breasts felt tight against the lace of her bra, her skin seemed to ache for the touch of his hands and she knew that her eyes were heavy-lidded and sensual, her pupils dark, telegraphing her feelings without the need for words.

But of course Zarek had no use for words. Even after two years apart, his senses were totally attuned to the signals she was unable to control. She saw his body still, the tension in the long muscles communicating a need that was like a visible force, reaching out to enclose her. His fierce, unblinking eyes were black as night, his touch on her face a brand that marked her out as his, and the hiss of his breath in between his lips was a sound that seemed to shiver all the way down her spine as she heard it.

'I missed things too,' he murmured, low and rough. '*Mou elipses*—I missed you—but most of all I missed this…'

And his head bent to take her mouth with his.

CHAPTER SEVEN

SHE had forgotten the sensation of drowning, Penny thought
hazily as Zarek's mouth closed over hers, the heat and
hardness of his kiss making her senses swim. She had forgotten how it felt as if a dark wave of sensuality was breaking
over her head, taking her down into the depths of passion
where she lost her last grip on control, gave herself up to the
sensation that possessed her.

One touch of Zarek's mouth on hers and she was once more
the naïve young virgin he had first taken to bed, at the mercy
of her hunger for him. A hunger that no other man had ever
been able to awaken in her. And waking up was what it felt
like. Waking from a deep dark sleep in which there had been
no sensation, no light, no warmth, no joy.

Now she was flooded with heat and hunger, a sensation
of coming back to life and seeing the glory of delight that
was possible.

Her head fell back under Zarek's kiss, her hands going up
to clutch at his arms, hold him near to her. Her lips opened
under the pressure of his and she felt the heated, sensual slide
of his tongue as he invaded the moist interior of her mouth.
No amount of wine could have more of a head-spinning effect

than the taste of him, no tantalising appetiser could stir her appetites as swiftly and as powerfully as it did.

'I have missed this,' Zarek muttered again, his voice thick and raw, his accent deep on every word. 'Missed it and thought about it so often at night. Longed for it. Hungered for it.'

He had gathered her up into his arms, crushing her tight against the heat and hardness of his body. Her head was pressed to his chest, feeling the wall of his ribcage under the soft cotton of his shirt. The race of his heart was like thunder in her ears and at the base of his strong neck she could see the heavy pulse that gave away how fiercely he was aroused. The force of his response sparked off an answering reaction in her own body. Moist heat pooled between her legs, in intimate evidence of the hunger he made her feel so easily.

'Zarek…'

His name felt strange on her tongue even though she'd used it before in the time since his sudden shocking arrival back in her life. But then it had been just a sound of shock. Now she was using it as a term of endearment, a recognition of something special, the name of her husband.

The man who had had the right to touch her as he was doing now. To stroke his hands over the shape of her body, sliding down her back, fingers tracing the line of her spine, until they splayed out over her hips, curved over the swell of her buttocks to press her even closer to him. His hips cradled her pelvis, the heat and swell of his erection hard against the softness of her feminine mound. Acting purely instinctively, she moved seductively against him, brushing against his arousal and hearing him groan low in his throat.

'*Gineka mou, gineka mou…Ise panemorfi.* You are so beautiful,' Zarek translated his muttered Greek, obviously needing her to understand.

Penny snatched in a shaken breath on a sound that even she was not quite sure whether it was a tremulous laugh, a gasp, or even an uncontrollable sob of response.

'I know. I know.' She whispered the words against his lips. 'You told me, remember?'

They had been some of the first words in his language that he had ever taught her.

*Gineka mou…*my wife. *Ise panemorfi.* You are so very beautiful.

And he had spoken them to her on their wedding day. Murmured them to her as they lay in bed. Whispered them in her ear as he took possession of her body for the very first time, took her virginity and made her his completely. And finally he had cried them aloud, in the heat of his passion and the throes of his climax as the thundering orgasm took them both right over the edge of the world, it had seemed, and out to spin in the wilds of uncharted space beyond.

At the time she had had no idea of what sexual fulfilment could possibly mean. She had dreamed and fantasised of course, yearned for Zarek's kiss, his touch. But she had had no concept of just how powerful a force of need could overwhelm her, the ecstasies that were within her reach when she abandoned herself to the skilled and knowing touch of her forcefully passionate lover. She only knew that she had given herself to him happily and willingly because she loved and had believed herself to be loved. She had thought that that was what made the difference.

Ten months of marriage had taught her all she needed to know. Ten months of marriage had given her time to learn, to discover her own latent sexuality and find herself as a sensual woman. A woman whose needs and desires were as hot and responsive as the man who made love to her each night.

And those needs, those hungers now rushed to the surface in a surge of demanding, stinging need in response to the caresses, the kisses of the man who had taught her everything she knew. Her one, her only lover.

She'd missed these sensations, missed him, and she couldn't hold back the ardent response that shuddered through her as she gave herself up to them for the first time in so long—far too long.

Zarek's hands were at her breasts, cupping their soft weight through the fine material of her clothing, making her moan aloud in a sound of hunger that she could just not hold back. It was not enough. She needed more. She needed the full sensation of his caress against her skin and she almost felt that she would have torn open the front of her dress to give him access if he didn't give her what she wanted.

But at the same time she wanted to use her hands to unfasten his clothing too. To wrench the buttons of his shirt from their fastenings, strip the fine cotton from his powerful torso, expose the muscled lines of his chest and shoulders to her hungry touch, her seeking mouth.

And Zarek was there ahead of her anyway. He needed no urging, no impatient encouragement as he used his mouth to ease the delicate straps of her green dress aside, fastening his teeth on one and tugging it down and over her shoulders. At the same time his hands were busy with the front of the garment, sliding it down over her straining, aching breasts to expose the creamy curves, the pink, tightly budded nipples that curled and hardened even more under the arousing caress of his knowing hands.

'Oh, Zarek…'

This time his name was a long, sighing cadence of delight as his thumbs swept over the swollen tips. The rough caress sent burning arrows of pure pleasure along every nerve pathway to centre in the most feminine core of her being, where they piled further hunger, built even more need on the yearning that was already driving her to total distraction. She couldn't take much more of this, couldn't take any more…the thought was like a beating refrain inside her head, making her feel as if her mind would blow apart if she was subjected to this onslaught of sensation for very much longer. She couldn't take much more and stay in one piece and yet she knew that if Zarek so much as considered stopping then she would disintegrate, would fall into pieces in a totally different way.

'I want you…'

She wasn't sure which one of them said the words first. The truth was that the declaration was torn from both of them in almost the same moment so that the rough-voiced assertion sounded as if there hadn't been two single people speaking it but one of them as a whole, both male and female proclaiming the overwhelming primal need that had them in its grip.

'I want you…' Penny managed again, her low, shaken voice sounding like an echo that had fallen from the very first pronouncement and was now fading away into a broken whisper, almost drowned out by the crash of the waves against the cliffs beyond the open door. 'I want you.'

'And you shall have me,' was Zarek's ardent response as he lifted her from the floor, swinging her up into his arms and carrying her swiftly from the room.

The hallway and stairs were still in almost total darkness but Zarek seemed to have eyes like a cat so that he didn't hesitate for a moment but strode swiftly up the stairs, even taking them two at a time at one point, in his haste to reach their bedroom. Kicking open the door, he hurried her across to the bed where he tumbled her down on the covers, coming down beside her in an instant.

'*Ise panemorfi...Ise panemorfi.*'

He was muttering the phrase over and over again, punctuating each word with a kiss on a different part of her exposed body. Her face, her shoulders, her arms, down the slopes of her breasts. And then, at last, at long, long last, his mouth closed, hot and hungry, over one tight nipple. Sharp teeth scraped it so gently for a moment, before he suckled hard to relieve the tiny pain, making her arch against him with a low, wordless cry of pleasure.

'Z-Zarek...'

His name was all she could manage as any thought and the ability to find coherent words were obliterated by the sheer force of the sensual storm that took her. Acting blind, she had managed to pull open his shirt, tug it part way off his shoulders, so that at least her hands could explore the warm, tight contours of his chest, tangle in the rough haze of black body hair that tickled her palms, curled around her fingertips.

Zarek's hands were dealing with her dress, taking it down further at the front, tugging it up at the skirt to expose her legs, the plain white knickers that were now her only covering apart from the band of bunched material at her waist. And they didn't last for long under the determined assault of those powerful hands that tore them apart as if they had been made of nothing more substantial than tissue paper.

She had barely time to gasp in shocked excitement when those wicked fingers, gentler now, were stroking through the dark curls he had exposed, finding the moist cleft between her legs, the tiny bud that pulsed with hungry need.

She was so aroused that the first intimate touch of his hand on her had her crying out and throwing her head back against the pillows, her eyes closed so that she could focus on the shock waves of pleasure that rocked her world.

'I missed this…' Zarek's rough mutter close to her ear echoed her own private thoughts and all the time that knowing hand teased and tormented her, building the desire to the point where it almost broke her, then easing back to take her away from the edge just for a moment. 'And I know you did too. Missed what we had together…'

Penny had no idea where the sudden change of mood came from. The abrupt and totally unexpected switch from blind and greedy passion to a new and very different frame of mind, one that shocked her out of the heated sense of oblivion into which she had fallen. It was as if someone had suddenly opened a window, letting in an icy rush of cold night air that feathered over her exposed skin, cooling her blood and making her shiver in shocked response. As if a cold, cruel voice had spoken out of the blue, and the words she heard inside her head had the force of a slap in the face, jolting her back to bitter reality with a rush.

Missed what we had…

Missed what we had…

And what had they had? Blazing passion, true—a burning physical desire that had blinded her to everything else. But nothing more. There had been nothing between them but sex. At least on Zarek's part.

And was she going to let him just walk back into her life—and into her bed again—without so much as an argument? When Zarek had left for the *Troy* she had known that she had never meant her wild and hurting threats that she would not wait for him. She'd told herself that if she stayed, then when he returned she had to stand up to him. That there had to be more to make this marriage work, her love alone wasn't enough to sustain it, and something was going to have to change.

Two years was a much, much longer wait than the few days she had been expecting, but her resolve needed to still be so much the same. More so if she was to be able to survive as Zarek's wife ever again.

Nothing would change if she gave in at the first kiss, the first caress.

'Zarek…' She tried to speak but it seemed that all strength had drained from her voice and nothing audible came out.

'Gineka mou…'

Zarek had no such trouble and as he pressed his mouth against her breast again his words were perfectly audible. As was the darkly possessive note in them.

*Gineka mou…*My wife.

He was staking his claim on her once more, using sex to do so. That was how he'd won her, how he'd held her blind and deceived for the first six months of their marriage. But then she'd learned the truth…

'No!'

This time she had no trouble in making herself heard. The cry of rejection was loud and clear, echoing round the empty house. In the same moment she tried to push at Zarek, push him away from her. Free herself from his possessive and dangerously enticing hold. His hands still caressed, his mouth pursed to press another kiss against her breast and she could feel the hot, moist touch of his tongue against her skin. Another moment and she would be lost again. Already she could feel the tidal waves of dark desire sweeping over her, threatening to drown out the frantic voice of sanity and self-preservation.

'I said *no!*'

With urgent, desperate hands, she pushed at him but he was too big, his powerful body too heavy for her attempts to move him. So throwing caution to the wind she resorted to desperate measures. Reaching out, she grabbed a handful of his black hair—two—twisted her fingers in it, refusing to let herself think about the silky slide of it in her grip, and tugged. Hard.

'*Gamoto!*'

She didn't have to know much Greek to understand that Zarek's violent explosion of sound was definitely a swear word. She only had to see the way his head came up, his eyes flaring sharply.

'What the…?'

'I said no!'

Surprise gave her an advantage she hadn't expected and with a frantic wriggle, another push, she was free of his confining weight, out of the bed and thudding onto the floor. Panic carried her halfway across the room, almost falling as she struggled to keep her balance and get as far away from him as possible so that he couldn't reach out and grab her, use his superior strength to hold her, keep her prisoner.

'What the hell…?'

If Zarek's eyes had been sparking irritation before, now they were positively incandescent. They burned with fury, turning a look on her that she felt really should have shrivelled her into a pile of dust where she stood, silhouetted against the window, the moonlight lighting her from behind.

'You…'

Zarek stopped abruptly, clearly fighting to bring himself under control. With an effort he drew in a long harsh breath between his gritted teeth and raked an angry hand through his hair, sweeping it back from his forehead so that the harsh white line of the cruel scar showed up so much more clearly in stark relief.

'What the hell is this?' he demanded again, his words

falling ragged and raw into the shocked stillness of the night. 'What sort of game—?'

'No game!' Penny put in frantically, suddenly terribly afraid that he might still consider this some risky sort of foreplay, designed to heighten anticipation, increase appetite, and decide to go along with what he thought she wanted.

She had had a narrow enough escape as it was, barely managing to escape before the dark seas of need had closed over her head completely, drowning her for ever. If he touched her again she didn't know if she had the strength to resist him.

'No game at all! I'm deadly serious...'

The look he flung at her almost totally destroyed what little was left of her self-control, but, heaving in a desperate breath, she forced herself to face him with as much strength and defiance as she could muster.

'This has gone far enough—too far. I don't want it. I don't want you.'

'Liar!'

It was low and deadly and this time his eyes burned molten with rejection of every word she'd said.

'You little liar. You wanted me every bit as much as I wanted you. You said so—'

'I was wrong...'

'And your body said so too. It's still telling the same story.'

A wild, contemptuous gesture in her direction emphasised the angry words.

'You can't deny—'

'Oh, but I can—I will!'

Her voice was pitched too high, too shrill. It sounded too despairing, too desperate to protect herself. Which was hardly surprising when she could barely bring her whirling senses back under any degree of control. Her pulse was still pounding in her veins, sounding like thunder in her head.

'You would?'

Cynical disbelief rang rough in Zarek's voice, making her shiver because she knew that she couldn't refute. He knew that she was lying and so did she.

'You'd deny this…'

Before she could even realise that he had moved he was at her side in three long strides. Hard hands clamped around her naked shoulders, bruising fingers digging into the skin as he swung her round in front of him. This way she faced the big full-length mirror set into the wardrobe on the opposite side of the room.

'You'd deny *this*?' Zarek repeated savagely. 'Look at yourself!'

Penny closed her eyes tight. she didn't want to look—didn't need to look. She knew what he meant; knew what she would see. But a rough shake of her shoulders forced her to open them again. When she did so the first thing she saw was Zarek's dark eyes looking over her shoulder, meeting hers in the glass. That was bad enough but the burn of something dangerous in that glittering stare made her drop her gaze and face her reflection squarely, wincing in embarrassment as she did so.

It was worse than she had expected.

The green dress was bunched up around her waist, her wildly disordered clothing exposing her breasts. The creamy flesh still marked with red as the result of his kisses, the abrasion of his late evening stubble against the sensitive skin. Her hair was a wild bird's nest around her face, tumbling in tangled chaos on to her shoulders. Her nipples were still hard and flushed with pink, faintly gleaming with the moisture left on them by his tormenting mouth.

Her breasts stung where they were now exposed to the air and rapidly cooling from the heated response of just moments before. And between her legs the throbbing need his deliberately provoking caresses had awoken and then stoked with every touch was still a burning torture of demand. One that made her feel it might actually drive her to lose consciousness from the agonising frustration of having to fight it. Just for a second she felt weak enough to sag back against Zarek's strength and support, but realised in time how appalling a mistake that would be.

'I mean—I can't deny that it happened. That I responded.'

It seemed that was not the response Zarek was expecting. The grip on her shoulders eased slightly, becoming loose enough for her to twist away. At least this way she didn't have to look at herself, or meet his darkly accusing eyes.

'I'd be a fool to try and do that—wouldn't I? I mean—look at me…'

No, that was a mistake. Bringing his eyes to her exposed body, reminding him of how she looked, how he had made her look, was not going to help her in this. With a flare of hot embarrassment flooding up into her cheeks, she tugged at the skirt of her dress with one hand, the top of it with another, both movements having very little practical effect.

'Here…'

To her total shock and consternation, Zarek moved across the room, snagged a blue silky robe from the back of the door, shook it out and held it open.

'What?'

'Put it on…'

At the sight of her wary-eyed hesitation, he muttered an imprecation in savage Greek.

'I am not going to harm you.'

'I know…'

Whatever else there might have been between them—or not—Penny knew Zarek was not was physically cruel or hurtful.

But these were not normal circumstances. She still had no idea at all what had happened to Zarek while he had been away. The whole time of his absence had started with the violence of the hijacking of the *Troy* by the pirates. Then there had been the ordeal of being held hostage in the tiny, enclosed boat, the bullet that had been meant for his head and had only by some miracle missed by inches.

And after that? That had all been in the very first week— God knew what had happened in the years afterward.

Oh, but the truth was that even when they had been together, she had never truly known him. She had married him in a rush, in the heat of the biggest crush she had ever had in her life. She had been wildly in love, with the emphasis on *wild*, but she had never really known the man she had married. That had been proved to her by later developments.

'I'm sorry—I know you wouldn't harm me under normal circumstances!'

It was meant to be a peace offering, a verbal olive branch, and although Zarek nodded in acknowledgement it didn't subdue the blaze in his eyes or ease the tension in his jaw and shoulders.

'Then cover yourself up and perhaps we'll be able to talk— *normally*.'

The bitterly cynical emphasis on the last word made Penny wince, as did the bleakly efficient way he was setting about restoring his appearance to—that word again—normality. The way he buttoned up his shirt, tucked it in where she had pulled it adrift at the waist, smoothed the disordered hair her clutching fingers had tangled, spoke very clearly of his instant withdrawal from her.

What had happened to the hot-blooded, fiercely passionate man who had carried her up to his bed just a short time before? Had he really existed? Or had she been deluding herself? Had that been just another sign of cool calculation on Zarek's part? Like the way he had decided to marry her in the past.

The way he had chosen her as the potential mother for his heirs.

CHAPTER EIGHT

SHIVERINGLY cold in spite of the warmth of the September evening, Penny stumbled across the room to where Zarek still held out the blue silk robe and pushed her arms roughly into the sleeves. It was all she could do not to snatch the robe away from him as he pulled it up around her shoulders, but the ordeal didn't take long. A moment later she was back over the other side of the room, dragging the sides of the robe together and belting it as tightly as possible around her waist. It was made of soft and thin material, so it was little use as protective armour against him, but at least she was covered and felt more secure that way.

'You never needed to armour yourself against me.' Zarek's drawl stunned her with its hint of dark amusement. Even more so with its uncanny echoing of the word in her own thoughts. 'And you never used to play games in bed—at least not those sort of games.'

'I wasn't playing any sort of game.'

'No?'

With the blue robe wrapped round her, Penny felt a little more secure and able to face his cold-eyed derision.

'I wasn't playing at anything. I know I responded—there was always that spark—OK, more than a spark—of passion between us.'

'As I recall, you couldn't keep your hands off me. And vice versa. But then I'm not the one denying the blatantly obvious.'

'I'm not denying it,' Penny persisted. 'I'd be a fool to even try. It's there, obviously it is—but that doesn't mean I'm going to act on it.'

Whatever else Zarek had been expecting, it was not that. His dark head went back sharply, his eyes narrowing till they were just gleaming slits in his tanned face.

'I'm not someone who just jumps into bed with any man in the first moment I see him, no matter how strong the provocation.'

He knew that. She saw the acknowledgement of it in his eyes even though he said nothing in response. She'd come to him a virgin and, in spite of an almost overwhelming longing to change that situation before then, she had been a virgin on their wedding night.

'I'm not just any man.'

'But I don't know you.'

'I'm your husband!'

It was a sound of fierce exasperation blended with total disbelief of what she was saying. Penny took several steps backwards, away from him, stopping short when she found that her back had come up against the wall. She could see from his face that he thought she had gone completely mad, right before his eyes, and even in her own mind her argument sounded weak and unsubstantial. But then he had got exactly what he wanted from their marriage. She wasn't yet prepared to open up her heart to him and confess the truth—that he wasn't the husband she needed.

She had more pride than to admit that until she knew more clearly exactly where she stood.

'So you keep telling me.'

'Are you saying you don't believe I am who I claim to be? What do you want—a DNA test?'

Penny flinched at the malign humour in his dark tones but, pushing her hands into the pockets of the silk gown and curling them into tight, defiant fists, she managed to find the strength to continue in spite of feeling that she was suddenly desperately fighting for her life.

'N-no—I don't need that.'

'Then start acting like you know me. I'm your husband—the man you married—and you damn well know it. And if you need any further confirmation—something we both know—then let me remind you that I am also the man who made sure that you—or at least an image of you—was added to the carving on our bed.'

One long tanned hand pointed back at the dishevelled bed they had just left.

'Yes—as a mouse!' Penny flung back at him.

She knew he was referring to the ornately carved wooden headboard that had been one of the wedding gifts at their marriage. Apparently these carvings were a tradition in the Michaelis family and were usually made up of symbols and images to represent the bride and groom, their families and elements from their lives. When the headboard had been given to Zarek and Penny it had all seemed to be about boats and the sea, with very little that related to her personally. When she had protested, Zarek had said that he would make sure she was added. She had come back from her wedding reception expecting at the very least to see a rose or two for her English nationality, or even a soaring oak tree as a play on her maiden name of Wood.

It had taken her a long time to find the tiny field mouse almost hidden in one corner of the ornate bed head.

'Was that what you thought of me? As a mouse? A creeping, sneaking, terrified little mouse?'

'Well, certainly not now,' Zarek replied dryly, strolling over to a chair by the window and dropping down into it. 'Right now you are—what is it that old film was called?— The Mouse that Roared.'

Was that actually a gleam of humour in the darkness of his eyes? Penny couldn't be sure and because of that she didn't dare risk rising to his teasing.

'You have changed, Penny.'

If only he knew how much.

'I've had to change—had to learn how to stand on my own two feet. One moment I was a new wife, embarking on a very different sort of life in an alien country—with in-laws who weren't exactly pleased to see me arrive in their home, but with my husband by my side to help me through. The next I was…'

Breaking off, she could only shake her head, twisting the tie belt of her robe round and round her fingers, tying it in knots and then tugging them free again.

'The next you were what?' Zarek prompted when she couldn't find the words to go on. 'You didn't seem to be struggling quite as much as you would have me believe. Certainly not with the in-laws.'

'You think so?'

Outrage had Penny letting drop the narrow belt as she put her hands on her hips and faced him defiantly.

'You want to try living with your stepmother complaining about every thing every minute of the day. With everything you do being wrong—and everything that dear Jason and Petros do is absolutely perfect.'

It was only when Zarek's mouth quirked up into an unexpected and totally unguarded smile that she realised just how rigidly he had controlled his features from the time he had arrived until now. Even when he had been intent on seducing her, no trace of true emotion had shown through the tight muscles, only the burn in his eyes giving away any sort of feeling. It had been almost as if he had been determined not to show anything. So now she felt her insides twist, her heart lurch as she recognised the unexpected softening in his face.

'I did,' he acknowledged dryly. 'I lived with that constant carping from the moment my father first brought Hermione home. And then when he married her and moved her and her sons into the house…'

He shook his head slowly, mouth twisting again at the memories.

'I was glad to escape to boarding school in England.'

'How old were you?'

Penny knew that her voice sounded slightly breathless because she was struggling with a tightness in her chest that came from the fact that Zarek had actually opened up about something in his past. When they had married he had always insisted that the past was irrelevant. That it was the here and now that mattered.

'Seven.'

'So young!'

At seven she had gone to the small village school just down the road. She couldn't imagine how it would have felt not to be able to go back home at the end of each long, tiring day.

'But I suppose you had Jason and Petros for company? No?' she questioned when Zarek shook his head again.

'They never went away to school. They had private tutors here on the island.'

Catching the sound of her swiftly indrawn breath, he switched on another smile, one that was totally different from before.

'I much preferred it that way. And if I could have stayed at school through the holidays I would have preferred that too.'

The words were flat, emotionless, but all the same Penny felt that she saw something of the reasons why Zarek had always been so totally set against his stepfamily, his unyielding resolve that they would never get their hands on Odysseus Shipping.

And that perhaps was some part of the explanation why he had been so determined on having a family—an heir—as soon as possible. But it did nothing to ease the sense of being used, seen not as a wife but as a womb to carry that child, which was how she had ended up feeling in their marriage. And that was why she had resorted to taking the contraceptive pill, the discovery of which had sent Zarek incandescent with rage just before he had left for the *Troy*.

'And your father?' she asked and once more Zarek shook his head.

'He gave Hermione whatever she wanted. He just wanted a quiet life and, to get that, he had to let her run things the way she wanted them.'

'Then you'll understand why I was ready to get out of here. You walk back in and assume that I've just been sitting here quietly, waiting for you to return. Perhaps doing a little embroidery to pass the time.'

The realisation that she had in fact been doing something like that made her heart skip a little uneven beat. She didn't really expect an answer to her question and she didn't get one. Instead Zarek continued to sit as motionless as a statue, even his eyes hooded and opaque.

'How do you know that I hadn't decided I'd had enough long ago and divorced you?'

'On what grounds?' Cool and swift, it had a bite as lethal as that of a striking snake.

'Desertion?' she parried sharply, refusing to let herself think of the way that he had never meant his marriage vows. Never intended to *love* and cherish. 'You haven't been in contact for two years.'

Something had changed. She couldn't tell quite what it was, only that something in the atmosphere in the room was suddenly very different. Zarek hadn't moved or spoken but everything about his long, still body communicated a new and very different form of tension.

'I believe that we have already established that I was hardly in a position to phone you or to send many text messages.'

The dry, slightly mocking words only added to the already strung-out way she was feeling, knocking her over from irritation into full-blown exasperation.

'When you were captured originally, perhaps! But you got away from them. That same week, if I have it right. And after that? There are two whole years with not a word, not a message. Nothing to let me know that you were still alive.'

'Perhaps that's because I didn't know that I was.'

'What…? What do you mean? That doesn't make sense.'

But even as she asked the questions Zarek moved at last, getting to his feet and prowling restlessly across the room to stand by the window, staring out at the now moonlit waves. And as she saw his hand come up to rub at his head, at the ugly scar that marked his temple, she felt her heart thud just once, hard and cruel, at the reminder that he had been literally just inches away from death. How long it would have taken him to recover from that she had no idea.

'I mean that for a long time even I did not know who I was,' Zarek said, still not looking at her so that he didn't see the way that her hands had gone to her mouth as if she could wish her foolish words back. 'When I hit the sea I had already blacked out. I have no idea how long I drifted. I was just lucky that I was eventually picked up by a man in his yacht. He took me back to his home in Malta.'

'Malta!'

Penny felt she might choke on the word. Was that where Zarek had been all this time? When she had been imagining all sorts of horrors, the thought of his lifeless body tossed into the ocean with a bullet in his head, he had been on that beautiful Mediterranean island.

So near and yet so far.

And what had he been doing all that time while she had been left stranded, neither a wife nor a widow? Not knowing whether to mourn him or to wait for him.

'Don't they have phones in Malta? Writing paper? Envelopes? A post office?'

That brought Zarek swinging round to face her, a faintly wry smile twisting his beautiful mouth in his shadowed face. That smile twisted a knife in her insides with its memory of how he had once looked, in the early days of their marriage, when he had been smiling at something she had said.

'I wouldn't have known who to contact. At the start, when I was unconscious and ill from exposure, I had no identification on me, no way of anyone knowing who I was. And when I did come round, I was no help.'

'Oh, come on…' Penny began, but then the full impact of just what he had said hit home to her and the words faded into nothing as her mind reeled in shock. 'Do you mean…? Are you saying…?'

'I'm saying I had amnesia—the wound on my head—the shock—exposure—any of it could all have caused it or added to the effect—but I couldn't remember a damn thing. I knew I was alive—I was male and…'

He threw up his hands in a gesture expressing resigned acceptance of defeat.

'That was it. So I couldn't help anyone by telling them who I was or who might be looking for me. I didn't know if I was married or single. If I had any family and where they were. I spoke English—that was what my rescuer spoke to me—but not Maltese. I also spoke French, Greek, Italian—so in which of those countries did I look for any clues?'

'Amnesia…'

Penny could only echo the word in a sense of shock and bewilderment. It was so obvious now that she knew. It explained so many things, which was a relief.

And it also took away that feeling of outraged injustice at the thought that she had been left abandoned, suffering the torment of believing him dead when all the time he had been alive and well and living in Malta.

Suddenly it was as if that sense of outrage had been all that had been holding her upright. As if the removal of the indignation had been like tugging a rug from under her feet, throwing her totally off balance. Was it possible that her own lingering anger and hurt at all that she had found out about him just before he had left for the *Troy* had coloured her judgement, making her see hurts where none was intended, cruelty where he had never planned any?

But all the same he had come back to the island incognito, if not in disguise. He had come in secret, concealed behind the big beard, the long hair. And he had set himself to watch her, to observe what she was doing. For how long? Just how many days—weeks—had he been there?

'Wh-when did you start to remember things?'

'Only slowly. I'm not sure if I fully recall everything yet. For perhaps the first year I didn't know anything. But occasionally I would have flashes of memory or dreams—'

He broke off abruptly as an unexpected sound interrupted his words. A sound that made Penny blush and made a rare, stunningly genuine smile of real amusement cross his face.

'What was that?'

'What?' It was an attempt at distraction, one that didn't work as her empty stomach growled again, more loudly this time.

'Are you hungry?'

It was so long—too long—since she'd seen that teasing smile on his face. And having seen it resurface, she felt she would do anything to keep it there. There had once been a time when they were happy together, even if, underneath it all, Zarek had only been pretending.

'A little,' she admitted. 'No—a lot…'

It was the first time she had sounded genuine, unconstrained, since she had leapt from the bed as if all the hounds of hell were after her, Zarek reflected. The first time she had sounded at all like the woman—little more than a girl—that he had married. And she pressed her hands to her belly as if somehow she could silence the growl of hunger that sounded once again.

'Me too, now,' he admitted, finding he could say it to this softer, younger-looking Penny. 'I haven't eaten all day.'

'Neither have I.'

She said it with a sort of astonishment that made him smile at her obvious sudden self-discovery.

'I didn't manage anything this morning because—the meeting was on my mind. And since then, well…' she shrugged, her expression becoming almost shame-faced '…things rather intervened.'

'They did. For me too.'

It seemed ridiculous to be having this rather inane conversation about food in the darkness of the late evening in the silence of the big house. Especially in the heated atmosphere that had been boiling between them earlier. But privately Zarek found that he was admitting he was actually rather enjoying it. It was a relief to have a slight lull in the tension and abrasive aggression of the rest of the day. The constant need to keep his focus on what was being said and how it was being expressed. After his investigations of the past weeks, the sense of always looking over his shoulder had become so much a part of his life that he was glad to let it drop for a while.

And not just in the time since he had rediscovered who he was. The worst thing about getting his memory back had been recalling the way that had been a part of his life for so long. Knowing that Hermione and her poisonous sons were always waiting and watching, just hoping for a chance to stab him in the back. They had tried their damnedest when his father had been alive, putting any barrier they could between him and his parent, and in the two years since Darius had died had re-doubled their campaigns in the hope of moving in on Odysseus Shipping.

And they had almost succeeded. If he had not walked in on the board meeting when he had…

But exactly what part had Penny played in that?

'Let me get you something.'

'There's no need…'

'Well, who else is going to do it, seeing as you've given the whole staff the night off?'

She made the comment sound light but he could still read the tension in her eyes, the faint quiver of her bottom lip. She obviously felt vulnerable and exposed alone in the house with him like this. Which was exactly how he wanted it. How he had planned it all the way along. Until he knew exactly what his lovely wife had wanted...

She had declared to his face that she and Jason were not lovers—had not been lovers. And he found that he believed her. How could she respond to him as she had just done if she had ever been intimate with his stepbrother? She had been as much at the mercy of frustrated hunger as he had felt after two long years away.

Which meant that the passion they had just shared still blazed between the two of them, though she seemed determined to deny it. For the life of him, he couldn't see why. Unless she had something else to hide.

And she had been good at hiding things. A sudden flash of memory reminded him of the way, the last time he had been in this room, he had planned to leave a gift, some of her favourite perfume, in a drawer in her dressing table for her to find while he was away. Instead, the perfume had ended up in the waste-paper basket, thrown there in a dark fury when he had found the packs of contraceptive pills...

For a moment the memory of the bitter disillusionment that had savaged him then came back to slash at him. He had married Penny because she had driven him half mad with wanting but also because she had seemed different. Because she had appeared to offer something so unlike the poisonous atmosphere of lies and greed. Because she had seemed innocent and open. So when he had found that she had been deceiving him all along, he had vowed that never again would he let a beautiful face, an innocent air, mislead him.

But, oh, dear heaven, she *was* lovely.

The sensual thought sprang from nowhere into his mind, knocking him sideways mentally, and very nearly physically.

It had such a force that he actually almost staggered under it, taking a single involuntary step to the side to steady himself as he did so. His body was still burning with the heated response that had seared through him such a short time before. He might have himself back under control but the hungry ache just would not go away and it left a throbbing bruised sensation along every nerve that still came close to making him want to groan aloud.

Now he knew why he had never been able to touch another woman in the time he had been away. Never had the inclination even though there had been plenty of opportunity, plenty of chances on offer to him. But even when he had still been struggling with his memory, when he hadn't yet recalled just who he was, some inner instinct had created a restraint that had held him back from taking advantage of any of them.

And, looking back, he knew that the only women who had ever interested him had shared his wife's sleek dark hair, her tall, willowy build and huge deep blue eyes. The brutal kick of sexual hunger that thought brought made him rush to force his mind onto other, less provocative matters.

'A meal would be welcome. As would a shower.'

He even managed a smile. It wouldn't hurt to be civilised for a while, even if the feelings he was burying behind the smile were very far from civilised and only just barely under control.

'The plumbing at the cottage was very much on the primitive side.'

The rush of relief into her eyes was one that set his teeth on edge. Did she really think that she had got away with it after all? That everything was now sweetness and light between them? If she did then she had no real recollection of the man her husband was. She had lost out on a lot when he had come home, her plans to leave and start a new life ruined by the fact that she could not have her husband declared dead as she had planned. He had rushed into a relationship with her once before and lived to rue the day he had met her. He was not going to let himself get trapped that way again. But he could afford to take things rather more slowly for a while.

'It must have been. Well, you can take this bathroom while I…'

Belatedly she realised how she sounded, the gracious lady-of-the-manor act she was putting on with a welcome guest. But he was no guest in his own home and whether he was actually welcome was something he had yet to finally prove one way or another. That burned in his gut so viciously that he knew it must show in his eyes, in the uncontrolled glare he turned on her suddenly smiling face.

It had her stumbling over her words, coming to an abrupt halt and snatching in a raw, ragged breath before she made herself go on in a very different tone altogether.

'I'm sorry—I mean—I'll use one of the other bathrooms. Of course.'

'Of course,' Zarek echoed dryly.

In the past they had shared many showers in the big luxurious wetroom that formed the en suite bathroom to the master suite in the villa. Long, indulgent showers that had often ended up with them back in bed at least once before they ever decided it was time to dry off and get dressed again. Now she looked as if she couldn't wait to get out of the room and…

Or did she? OK, she looked edgy as hell, already moving a careful step and then another towards the door. But there was a darkness in her eyes that didn't fit with the image of careful retreat. It was the sort of darkness that he suspected was still in his eyes too, making his pupils huge, swallowing up all the colour of his irises. It was the darkness of awareness, of arousal. And just to see it made his throat ache with the effort of holding back everything he wanted to say.

The way her arms were folded tight under the soft swell of her breasts, pushing them up and forward, sent his blood pulsing hot and heavy through his head. And her hands curved to cup their softness in a way that made the bite of sensual jealousy a torment he could barely keep under control. He wanted to stride forward, to tug her arms away from their defensive position, hold them prisoner high above her head, keep them there while he plundered her mouth with his, tasting her sweetness, taking her lips' hungry response into his own.

The blue robe might be fastened tight around her slender frame in a way that spoke of determined defence, of protection from his touch, from his kisses, but it was no defence against his eyes or his thoughts. He could still see the outline of the rucked up dress, the pleats of cotton at her hips and waist. But below that the soft silk clung lovingly to the fine curves of her thighs, the shadowed place between them, reminding him, sharp as a cruel knife, of how close he had been to being able to bury himself in her and find the heaven of release he sought. The release of oblivion in ecstasy.

It was a cruel irony that he had only just come to remember his life and there was so much of it that he wished he had never recalled. An even crueller stab of fate was the fact that Penny had been the first memory to return. Thoughts of her had been there in flashes, haunting his dreams, just out of reach, even before he had known who she was. It had been the need to find her that had driven him to try harder and harder to remember.

And then, when he had recalled just who she was, he had felt that burn of disillusionment all over again.

'If you need a change of clothes…' Penny's voice broke into his thoughts.

'It's all right…'

This was something he had already decided he would have to concede on. He had been away for two years. The reports had had him dead. Anyone—everyone—would have thought that it was a crazy thing to do to hang onto his clothes for that long. After his mother had died, even his own father had had to acknowledge that, adore her as he had, he couldn't keep his first wife's wardrobe when she had been gone six months.

'I understand if there's nothing here.'

'No—'

She had crossed to the wardrobe that had always been his, was fumbling with the handle. Pulling it open, she stood back so that he could see. The sight of every item of his clothing still hanging neat and straight just as he had left them over two years before had an effect like a punch to his guts, driving all the breath from his body.

'You kept them…'

But that had her lowering her face as if in embarrassment, brushing off his comment with an awkward little flick of her head.

'You know where the towels are…'

She almost ran from the room, leaving him staring after her, his mind see-sawing sickeningly as he tried to adjust to what had just happened.

She had kept all his clothes. In spite of the fact that she had been told he was dead, she had kept all his clothes as carefully and as well cared for as she had done when he was there. She hadn't cleared them out or packed them away, but had kept them here, in their bedroom. The room in which she still slept.

So what did that mean?

But he had seen her with Jason that first night. Seen the way she had run into his stepbrother's arms. And heard her…

'I want to get away from here, start living again. I'm tired of treading water… I can't inherit unless we have Zarek's death declared and legalised. So let's do that. Let's put it all behind us…'

And then, just as he reached the door this morning, that final, dismissive toast she had made, obviously with Jason in mind.

'The king is dead. Long live the king.'

So how did that square with the same woman who had kept every item of clothing he possessed for the time he had been gone? Did this mean that Penny had actually been hoping that he would come back?

In which case, why the hell had she bolted from his bed as if his touch appalled her?

Shaking his head, Zarek headed for the bathroom, discarding his clothes as he went.

He had taken his time about coming back, had sent a private investigator to check out the situation here on Ithaca first, before he had even made the journey from Malta and then moved onto the island incognito because he had wanted to watch and see for himself. Because, face it, the return of his memory had brought with it bad memories as well as good. Memories of feelings that the intervening two years could only have added to, made worse, dug in deeper.

And the woman he had come back to—the wife he had found waiting for him—was not at all what he had expected. For a start, he had never expected her to be here at all.

Turning on the shower full force, Zarek stepped under the rush of water and let it beat down on his head.

In fact there was just one way in which she was just the same as when he had left. And that was that she was the sexiest woman he had ever seen. The woman who only had to walk into a room to crank the heat up by one hundred degrees. Whose smile was an enticement to seduction. The woman who could make him burn with heat and hunger with one look, one word in her beautiful voice falling from her sexy soft lips.

She was a temptation strong enough to distract him from the way he really needed to be thinking, the things he had wanted to find out before he took up his old way of life again. His marriage was going to be so very different this time, or it was not going to exist at all.

But even as he told himself that the all-too-familiar heavy tightening in his groin warned him of what just thinking about Penny could do to him. The sort of reaction that stopped him thinking, drove the blood away from his brain and down to other, much more basic parts of his body. He'd already almost been caught that way once tonight. And thinking, not responding, was what he needed to do.

With a heavy sigh he reached up and turned the control on the shower to *cold* and forced himself to stand under it for far, far longer than he needed to get clean.

CHAPTER NINE

'THAT was wonderful, thank you.'

Zarek pushed his plate away from him, reached for his wine glass, and leaned back in his chair to sip at the golden-toned liquid with a sigh of contentment.

'It's so long since I tasted baked feta with peppers that I had almost forgotten how much I enjoyed it. And baklava…I didn't know that you knew how to make it.'

'Marta taught me,' Penny said, referring to the cook who usually ran the villa's kitchen with a rule of iron. 'I've been having cooking lessons with her—for something to do.'

She didn't add that she had specially learned how to make the simple dish and others like it because her instructor had told her that they were Zarek's favourites. She'd already given far too much away by revealing that she had kept all his clothes in the wardrobes since the time of his disappearance.

'So that's how you spent your time.'

'Part of it anyway.'

Once again Penny couldn't look at him but fixed her eyes on the dark line of the horizon. Even after ten o'clock at night it was still warm enough to sit out on the terrace beside the swimming pool and that was where she had served the quick and simple meal she had put together for them after she had emerged from the shower.

She hadn't stayed under the water for long. Once safely in the sanctuary of a bathroom belonging to another bedroom, at the far end of the landing from the master suite she and Zarek had once shared, she had been quick to strip off the blue silk robe, tossing it onto the bed and then freezing in horror at the sight that confronted her in another full-length mirror.

'Oh, my... No!'

Had she really looked such a shocking mess? With her dress dragged down and pushed up, actually torn in one place, she looked more like the victim of an assault than a passionate lover happy to give herself to the man she adored. Her underwear had disappeared, lost who knew where, and her hair was a complete bird's nest falling in wild and knotted disarray around a shock-pale face. Even the untypical light traces of make-up that the thought of today's dreadful board meeting had driven her to put on were smudged and smeared around her eyes, the soft tinted lipstick totally kissed off.

'No!'

Penny put her hands to her face, covering her eyes to block out the sight, then almost immediately snatched them away again. She couldn't bear to stay like this a moment longer. A long, hot shower would make her feel better, restore some sense of balance, repair her damaged self-esteem.

At least that was what she hoped for. What actually happened was that as she removed and discarded what little was left of her clothing all she could think of was the way that it had felt to have Zarek's urgent hands on her dress, snatching aside the straps, dragging her skirt up high to expose her legs... She could almost still feel his touch everywhere on her skin, on her face, her breasts...her thighs. Somehow those hungry fingers had seared a path over her flesh, one that would not vanish even when she was many metres away from him, separated from his presence by the thickness of several walls.

Even diving under the shower and turning it on full force hadn't helped. The heat of the water had followed the path of the heated touch, trickling between her breasts, sliding down to the dark curls between her legs, along her thighs... Making her freeze under the rush of the water as she felt it pound down on her head, seeming to thump out the syllables of Zarek's name against her skull. Over and over again without a pause.

Za—rek. Za—rek... Until she could bear it no longer but lurched out of the shower, water stinging her eyes. She had no way of knowing if it was the flow from the shower or the tears that threatened, only that she was half blinded by it, groping roughly for her towel before snatching from the rail at it and rubbing her face hard.

How was it possible that she had gone into the shower to feel clean, to wash away the scent of Zarek's body on hers, the feel of his touch, and yet now she felt worse than before, tainted, marked for ever? It was as if his caresses had been a brand, his kisses scarring her for life. She would never be free of the darkly sensual hold he had over her, the fetters of sexuality that had bound her to him from the very first.

And was that all that it was? she couldn't help wondering now. She had fallen head over heels for Zarek when she had first met him, and she had truly believed herself in love at first sight. But had it been anything more than a hugely powerful crush, the first stirrings of her female sexuality? She hadn't known what sexual desire really meant and so she had only thought of the way she had felt for Zarek in terms of love and giving her heart.

But her time married to this man had taught her that he, at

least, was capable of claiming her as his in purely sexual terms. Of wanting her only for the wild and white hot passion that flared between them every time they touched. Every time they kissed. He had wooed her, won her, seduced her, married her, made her his, without a single trace of love for her. He had wanted her in his bed, to warm and satisfy his body and to create an heir for the company that was really the only thing that touched his heart, or what part of a heart he actually possessed.

'I married you for a child!' The last angry words he had flung at her before leaving for the *Troy* came back to haunt her once more. 'If you want this marriage to continue then that is non-negotiable.'

A sensation like the trickle of something slow and icy slipped down her spine at the thought. And that sense of creeping cold was made all the worse by staring out at the moonlit sea and remembering all those other nights she had sat out here on the terrace, doing exactly that. Then she had had to fight so hard against the nightmarish thoughts of Zarek's lifeless body tossed overboard from the pirates' boat and left abandoned in the water. Just the memory she had of those thoughts made Penny shiver convulsively in spite of the warmth.

'Cold?' Zarek shocked her by the speed and focus with which he reacted, turning his attention—the attention she had believed was fixed on the view before them—onto her in the space of a heartbeat.

'No—not really,' she managed on an awkward laugh. 'Someone just walked over my grave.'

Then, when his dark brows drew together in a frown of confusion and incomprehension, she had to force herself to continue and explain the superstition.

'When you get a shiver like that it's said to mean that someone somewhere is walking over the spot where you're going to be buried. It's just an old wives' tale. I think the scientific explanation is that the shiver is a response to the release of stress hormones.'

She was rambling and betraying her nervousness by doing so. She could see it in the darkness of Zarek's eyes, shadowed in the flickering light of the candles she had set on the table around them. He was back to watching her too closely for comfort and the steady, intent observation he subjected her to made her shift uncomfortably in her seat.

'And are you?' he asked at last, lifting his wine glass to his lips again but not swallowing as he studied her over the top of it. 'Stressed, I mean.'

'Of course I am!'

This at least she could answer with total honesty, for a moment or two anyway. She still found it almost impossible to believe that he had come back from the dead. That he was here, sitting with her in the warmth of the evening with the sound of his breathing in her ear, the scent of his skin in her nostrils.

'Why wouldn't I be stressed? I started this morning as I have done for the past two years, thinking that I was alone—a widow—that my husband was dead. And then suddenly the door opens and there you are—large as life and twice as ugly. And—and…'

'And?' Zarek prompted when she stumbled over the words, unable to go on. Setting his glass down on the wooden table top, he leaned towards her, elbows resting on his thighs, chin supported on his hands. 'And?'

He was too close. Too dangerously close in every way. She could see the way that his chest rose and fell with each breath, the shadow at his jaw line of the growth of that black beard even though he must have shaved only that morning. This close, and looking into his eyes, she could see how they were not totally dark but the deep brown was flecked with gold, like sparks flying up from a fire. And the scent of his body was like some spice in her nostrils, making her blood heat, her heart pound.

'And now my life is upside down and inside out and I don't know where I'm going or who I am.'

'My wife.'

He inserted the words with smooth precision, like sliding the point of a stiletto into her ribs, so smoothly and easily that at first, at the start, she didn't actually feel any of the pain it was inflicting on her.

'You are my wife.'

It was so calm, so controlled, so totally sure that that was all that mattered. And the absolute certainty, the note of dark possessiveness, made her skin chill once more, the tiny hairs at the back of her neck lifting in tension as she managed to control another of those shivers this time.

'Nothing has changed.'

'Oh, but it has!'

Talking with Zarek now was rather like skating over a deep, murky pond that was just covered with thin ice. She was sliding every which way, unable to quite get her grip on what was really happening, while all the time being aware that under the ice were the coldest, blackest, most dangerous depths, just waiting for the moment that her foot went through the surface and she tumbled in. Then she had the desperate feeling that the waters would close right over her and the icy cold would steal all her breath away and leave her to drown.

'Things have to have changed. It's been two years since I saw you—a lot has to have happened in that time. Two years in which I don't know where you've been, who you've been with, what has happened to you.'

'I could say the same for you.'

Was that darker note that threaded his voice the result of the same sort of careful control she was imposing on herself, the fight not to let the discussion tumble over into the anger that had destroyed them the last time? Or was it one of warning, telling her she was treading on treacherous ground?

'Oh, I've just been here, all the time. But you...'

'All you have to do is ask.'

Could it really be that simple? But life with Zarek had never been simple anyway. So why should it start being so now, with the weight of the complications of his disappearance added to the way things had been before?

Ask. OK, then...

'You said you had amnesia. You didn't remember anything?'

'Not a thing.'

Was she imagining things or had he actually leaned just a little closer? She was drowning in his eyes, her senses seduced by the warm, clean scent of him. But she couldn't allow herself to be enticed that way. That was how she had fallen into love—her juvenile childish love—with him at the beginning. She had to hold onto her heart until she knew if it was safe to give it ever again.

'So what was it that started to bring your memory back to you?'

He took just a moment too long before answering her. The space of perhaps two heartbeats instead of one in a way that set her even more on edge. But his answer when it came was calm, and apparently open enough.

'Believe it or not, it was those damn pirates who helped to break down the walls my mind had built around it. I couldn't believe that I was having images of an attack, hearing the word *pirates* in the twenty-first century. And so I started to look things up, track down stories about pirates in the press, on the Internet. At first it was like looking for a needle in a haystack.'

Needing to break the almost mesmeric hold his closeness had on her, Penny forced herself to sit back, reach for her glass.

'But then one name kept going round and round in my head—the *Troy*… Careful.'

The last word was a warning as Penny swallowed too quickly, too awkwardly, and almost choked on her wine. She had been hoping for another name—her own name. The name of his wife. But no, the first things that had come back to him were connected with his company.

'You never could handle retsina,' Zarek said in mild amusement. 'In fact I always thought you hated it.'

'It wasn't to my taste at first,' Penny acknowledged. 'But I have to admit that I've grown to like it better.'

'Another of those things that have changed while I've been away.'

'Well, you wouldn't expect everything to just come to a halt—stay there, frozen in ice because you weren't here.'

Pure nerves had pushed the wild words from her tongue. And she knew what was twisting those nerves into painful knots so that she couldn't think straight.

'Of course not.'

'Of course not!' Penny snapped. 'We couldn't just give up on things. Life had to go on. For everyone. I mean, even…'

'Even…?' Zarek prompted when her throat closed up and she couldn't finish the name.

Penny reached for her glass again, took another fortifying sip of wine. Nerves had made her slip on the words, but suddenly she was determined to have this out. Time it was out in the open and faced.

'Even for bloody Odysseus Shipping.'

Oh, she had his attention now. If she thought that nearly black gaze had been focused before, now it had the burn of a laser so that she expected her skin to actually scorch where it rested.

It was too much to see the sudden change from stillness to attention. To watch his face change, the sudden light of interest in his eyes.

But, "Bloody Odysseus Shipping?" was all he said and his tone was quite mild, enquiring. 'You were desperate to get rid of it,' he added in the same sort of tone.

'Is that so impossible to believe?'

Pushing her chair back with an ugly scraping sound on the stone-tiled terrace, she got hastily to her feet and reached for his empty plate. Stacking it on top of her own, she winced inwardly at the crashing sound it made. She wasn't deliberately clattering them together, it just sounded that way. Her hands weren't as steady as she wanted and she cursed how much they gave away of her inner turmoil.

'I mean, I'm no hot-shot businesswoman. I'm a secretary—a very junior secretary at that. And when a company loses its chairman to sudden death—an accident at sea—and there is no one ready and trained to take his place, then apparently the values of shares waver—people wonder about their connections with the firm. Didn't you hear? I mean, I assume that you did a lot of investigating, checking on facts—looking into things before you came back to Ithaca. Just so that you knew what was going on.'

She actually paused and looked up at him, waiting for his answer. Not that she needed it. She knew already that he must have checked out all the details of what was happening on Ithaca before he had even thought about coming home. That was the sort of man Zarek was. He never made a move until he had all the facts.

'You didn't know!' she exclaimed as his head went back in shock. 'You really didn't find out about that?'

'I knew.'

Zarek's confirmation was a low growl as she made herself turn and head towards the kitchen with the dirty plates. She wouldn't allow herself to look back but she heard the pad of his bare feet on the tiles as he came up behind her.

At least the simple task of loading the plates and cutlery into the dishwasher meant that she could keep her back to him, focusing hard on the job in hand. But all the same she felt as if she could sense the tension coming off him in waves and directed at the back of her head, so sharp that it almost penetrated her skull.

'Then you'll understand why it felt like a millstone round my neck. And all the time I had Hermione and your stepbrothers on my back too. Telling me that nothing I did was right. That the company needed a man in control. So, yes, in the end I gave in. I'd had enough. I was going to walk away, go back to England. Start my life over again. Yes, I know you never wanted them to have the company, but what else could I do? It's not as if I had a child whose inheritance I had to fight for too.'

Too late she realised just what she had said, the minefield into which she had wandered. And the silence from behind her was so deep, so intense that she could practically feel it closing around her, sealing off her lungs, taking the breath from her body.

'No, you made sure of that.'

His voice had turned to ice. Icy shards that seemed to slash at her exposed and vulnerable skin.

'You knew I wanted a child. You led me to believe you wanted one too.'

Washing-powder tablet…rinse aid… Penny forced herself

to focus on the mundane details to stop her mind going into meltdown as she hunted for an answer.

'I didn't want your heir.'

She could answer him this way while she had her back to him and he couldn't see her face. It meant that she couldn't see his expression but that hardly mattered. It was much more important that he didn't know her answer for the half lie that it was. She hadn't wanted only to provide him with an heir, but the thought of a small baby with Zarek's black hair and deep brown eyes almost destroyed her. Her eyes were blurred with focusing on the front of the dishwasher so fiercely rather than let any tears form.

'But that was why we married—why I became your husband.'

Slamming the dishwasher door shut—the noise and force deliberate this time—Penny pushed herself up from the squatting position and pressed the start button fiercely.

He was leaning against the worktop, arms folded across his powerful chest, but the tension in the long body showed the position to be anything other than the relaxed one it appeared to be.

'But there's so much more to being a husband than just declaring it.'

Did something change in those eyes or was it just the flicker of the candlelight throwing a different set of shadows into them?

'What was missing? Was I cruel to you? Did I treat you badly—not give you everything you wanted?'

'You gave everything I could have dreamed of.'

If they were talking about material things. But from the moment that she had known how much she needed his love, then marriage, his beautiful homes, all the riches he had were as nothing compared with what she wanted most in all the world. And she had more pride than to beg for something he couldn't give her.

'And yet you didn't want to stay—you didn't want a child.'

Just as she couldn't read his face, she couldn't interpret his tone.

'We didn't have a marriage to bring a child into. A child has the right to have two parents who are happy to be together, and not just because of the life they had created between them.'

Two parents who loved each other.

She'd finished drying her hands on a towel and now she tossed it down onto the marble surface beside the sink. She'd prevaricated for as long as she could, avoided meeting his eyes until she could do so no longer. If she didn't turn now and look him in the face it would be so obvious that she was avoiding him that she would not be able to dodge it any more.

'I was wrong to marry you. My parents married just because I was on the way and it was a terrible mistake. They tore each other apart—and I was always caught in the crossfire.'

'We didn't even get that far,' Zarek murmured dryly.

'No—because I realised I should never have said yes in the first place.'

'So why did you stay when I was declared missing?'

'Someone had to hold things together. I discovered that you had left everything to me in your will. And there was always just the possibility that you might come back.'

'And now that I am back?'

'I really don't know.'

Simple honesty was all that she was capable of. In spite of the sleep she had had earlier that day she was suddenly desperately tired. It was as if the tension that had been holding her upright and keeping her going in all the time that Zarek had been away had now totally evaporated, taking with it her spirit and the strength of her spine. Her mind seemed hazed, her thoughts muddied.

'You don't know why you married me?' Zarek questioned sharply, throwing her even further off balance.

How was she expected to answer that without bringing the L word into things? Right now, attack seemed the better form of defence.

'Don't you think it's a little late to be asking that now? It never occurred to you to ask it when you were about to put a ring on my finger? Well, no, I don't suppose you did. Because for you it was all cut and dried, wasn't it? A cold-blooded business deal. You wanted me and you wanted a child. Marry me and you'd get both.'

Zarek shifted his weight from one hip to the other, but apart from that his expression remained unchanging.

'Not all such deals are cold-blooded.'

'No, of course not—we were pretty hot-blooded most of the time. And that gives you the reason why I married you. Great sex.'

When he dared to frown as if he needed more explanation she lost her grip on her tongue and really let him have it.

'I was twenty-two. You're pretty gorgeous—and rich. What's not to like?'

'Yes, there was that.'

'There definitely was.'

Somehow the defiance she dredged up from deep inside her made it easier than she thought to face that dark-eyed gaze.

'But while you've been away I've had time to grow up. And…and…'

Watching him wipe the back of his hand across his face, she found she was stumbling over her words. If she was tired then he looked drained, and she recognised the way that he pressed his fingers to the scar at his temple as a warning sign.

Looking at him more closely, Penny saw the shadows under his eyes, the faint cloudiness in the polished jet gaze. She thought that she knew how he felt. It was now well past midnight and she felt as if she had lived through several lifetimes in less than twenty-four hours. Right now she felt as if she was losing her grip on being able to control where the conversation went and what, underneath it all, it might mean.

'But I don't think now is the time to discuss it. It's been a long day. And we've both had so much adjusting to do since you came back.'

Dear heaven, was it only this morning? Just a few short hours before and yet she felt as if he had been back for ever. As if he had never been away. But he *had* been missing and that had had such an effect on her life that she had no idea quite when she would feel as if her existence was back under her control once more.

'We do need to talk more. But not tonight. It's late—and I'm—I'm tired.'

She accompanied the words with a stretch and a yawn to emphasise them but the truth was that she didn't have to put on any sort of a show. Now that she thought about it she was worn out, aching with tiredness right through to the bone, her head spinning nauseously.

Or perhaps it was the result of the stress of the day. A long day of trying to adjust to all that had happened, a day of shocks and bewilderment that had kept her feeling raw and on edge with every hour that passed.

CHAPTER TEN

SHE didn't expect that Zarek would allow himself to be diverted but to her surprise he nodded his head and stepped backwards towards the door.

'You're right. It is late, and I'll admit that I'm looking forward to sleeping in my own bed after all this time.'

Perhaps it was her own fatigue, or perhaps it was the way that they went up the stairs, Argus trotting beside her and Zarek switching off the lights behind them as he mounted the stairs, that blurred Penny's mind. They had done this so many other times in the past, when they had been married. Wandering upstairs in companionable silence at the end of the day, having shared a meal, a glass of wine and now heading for bed. But it was not until she reached the wide landing and turned towards the bedroom that reality hit home again reminding her of the truth of how things really were and making her stumble slightly, banging into the wall as she fought to keep her balance.

'Careful.'

Zarek put a hand out to support her, taking hold of her elbow and helping her to straighten up.

'Thank you.'

It was stiff and tight, the muscles in her throat clenching

in response to the feel of the heat of his palm against her skin, the burn of his touch along every nerve. In flashes of memory the scene in the bedroom earlier that night came back to haunt her, overlaid by older but no less vivid memories of the nights that Zarek had taken her to bed in the past. During their marriage. Starting with the heated passion of their wedding night that had left her weeping with joy and disbelief that such stunning passion could ever exist.

And now Zarek clearly expected that he would share her bed again. That they would sleep together in the wide soft marriage bed with its huge, ornately carved wooden head-board. And after his casual, 'Yes, there was that,' that was more than she could bear.

Coming to a halt before she actually reached the master suite door, she half turned towards Zarek and tried for what she hoped was an appeasing smile.

'I'll get you some clean towels and bring them to your bedroom. The blue suite is made up and ready.'

'The blue suite?'

Appeased was the last thing Zarek looked. His black brows drew together in an angry frown and the flash of something dangerous in the depths of his eyes made her legs tremble beneath her.

'I think not.'

'Oh, but…'

Protesting was a mistake. As was thinking that he was ever going to be persuaded on this one. Ruthless rejection of what she had planned was stamped in hard, cruel lines on his face, burning in that cold-eyed glare that he turned on her.

'Oh, but nothing. Not if you are trying to say that you think I should sleep elsewhere.'

His hand was already on the door, twisting the handle with

a force that spoke of the anger he was working to hold in check. But what made Penny's stomach tense and twist itself into tight, painful knots was not the thought of the dark fury he might feel but the demonstration of the ruthless power he was determined to exert to control it. The force of will it spoke of made her quail at the thought of it being used against her.

And which way would it be used? Earlier today he had wanted to take her to bed and she had been unable to resist. Only at the last minute had common sense reasserted itself, the much-needed sense of self-preservation kicking in to make her react in the rational way at last. If Zarek turned the sheer power of his seductive persuasion on her once more she might not be able to hold out this time.

Just the memory of the feeling of drowning in his kisses, in his touch, gave her the sense of going down for the third time. She could feel the dark heated waters of sensuality swirling about her dangerously once again.

'Where else would I sleep, *glikia mou*?'

The bite on the last two words took them to a point light years away from any real term of affection.

'This is my home, this is my bedroom. My bed. The bed I have dreamed of sleeping in again ever since I realised just who I was. There is nowhere else I intend to sleep tonight— or any other night.'

And there was no way at all she could refute that argument even if she dared to try.

'So—what about me?'

'What about you?'

The coolly assessing stare he turned on her moved from the top of her head, down to her toes where they curled nervously on the polished wooden floor, then swept back up again to linger on her uneasy face, looking straight into her frowning eyes.

'Where—where am I expected to sleep?'

'Expected?'

There was a dark note of mockery in that single drawled word, one that scraped over her nerves like the sound of fingernails on a blackboard, making her wince inwardly.

'I expect nothing from you, *agapiti mou*. I would be all kinds of a fool if I did. But as to where you should sleep—'

If the faint shrug of one shoulder was meant to be casual then it failed completely. As Penny suspected it was meant to. Instead she was sure that it was an indication of the fact that he didn't give a damn one way or another.

'The normal place that a wife sleeps is at her husband's side.'

'Normal!' Penny's anger was like a red haze in front of her eyes.

Once again Zarek was staking his claim to everything as he had been doing from the moment that he had walked back into her life that morning.

Back into *his* life. Into his house.

His room. His bed.

His wife.

And as his wife she was expected to warm his bed because that was what was normal. For normal read that Zarek would get what he wanted.

'We never had a normal marriage. And even if we had, you've been gone a long time. Long enough for you to be…'

No, her tongue wouldn't frame the word and she choked to a halt, watching the black frown that snapped his dark brows together.

'Long enough for what?' He pounced on the words like a hunting big cat on its prey. 'For me to be *what*?'

Something in her face gave her away and she saw those brilliant eyes narrow until they were just hard slits in a drawn face where white lines of anger and rejection were etched sharply around his nose and mouth.

'Oh, no, lady,' he said with savage control, the bite of the icy fury in his voice lashing against her skin so that she shivered in miserable reaction. 'You are not going to accuse me of being unfaithful to you. I respected my marriage vows even when I did not know that I had made them.'

'All that time—on Malta…?'

'All that time. Even though there was temptation.'

Of course there had been temptation. Zarek was a gorgeous man. A glorious, devastating specimen of manhood. Wherever he was, women were drawn to him like moths to a flame. He had only to direct one burning glance from those stunning, heavy-lidded eyes or flash a single wide, brilliant smile and every breathing female within reach was reduced to a molten pool of honeyed sensual response.

'So you're saying…'

'Not saying.' Zarek's delivery was brutal. 'Telling you. I have never broken my marriage vows to you.'

Could he really mean it? Mean that there had been no one else. Not even when he hadn't known who he was, whether he was married or not?

'And you expect me to believe that?'

'Why not? I believed you.'

It was so unexpected it hit her like a slap in the face, making her reel back.

'I thought you were dead,' was all she could manage.

Zarek pushed one hand roughly through the shining darkness of his hair, shaking his head slightly.

'You thought I was dead. You believed you were a widow. Even if you had met someone new while I was away. I couldn't expect you to wait for ever.'

'But I didn't—' Penny began, but Zarek persisted, talking across her as if she hadn't spoken.

'I understand that Jason saw an opportunity to step into my shoes, in more ways than one. And I have no doubt that he was fully prepared to use you to do just that. If you'd let him.'

'He helped me run the company. I certainly didn't have the experience to do so.'

'And he was kind.' Zarek pronounced the word as if it were a foul, bitter taste in his mouth and suddenly Penny's temper flared out of control.

'Yes, he was kind—and because of that I might have been tempted. So perhaps you might like to stop and think about your part in that.'

Oh, that had got his attention. His head went back as if she had slapped him in the face and if his eyes had seemed to burn before now they practically seared off a fine layer of her skin, leaving her raw and unprotected underneath.

So raw that she no longer cared what she said or how she said it. She only knew that she had had enough for tonight. That she couldn't go on but she needed to escape to somewhere dark and private. To some silent sanctuary where she could lick her wounds for a while and try to come to terms with everything that had happened today. To face up to everything that had changed—and everything that had still remained so agonisingly the same. Perhaps after some time alone, time for thought, she might just be able to face whatever came next. Whatever the future—and Zarek—decided to throw at her.

'The reasons why I might want someone who could be *kind* rather than a man who is so determined to lay claim to his home, his bed—*his wife*. To have them all under his control like his precious company. Someone who thinks that he can walk back into my life and demand that the woman he married should be at her husband's side, in her husband's bed, whether she wants to be there or not.'

But she'd overstepped the mark there. From the way Zarek's lips thinned, his jaw tightening ominously, she knew exactly what was coming even before he shot the question at her viciously.

'And are you saying that you have no desire at all to be in my bed? Are you saying that what happened between us earlier this evening was totally what I *demanded*? That it was simply you *under my control*—with no say in what was going on? That it was not what you wanted at all?'

'No—yes…'

Oh, how did she answer that? The truth was that she had wanted it. Wanted it until she had felt she was going to shatter into tiny pieces with the yearning that was eating her up inside. And yet at the same time it was exactly what she did *not* want. The sensual enticement Zarek offered was such a blend of temptation and danger that it would destroy her if she gave into it as she had done when she had rushed into marriage with him without thinking about the possible consequences. But at the same time, somewhere deep in her heart she had the terrible feeling that it would also devastate her if she never knew it again, never experienced just once more the sexual magic that Zarek could bring to her body, the total ecstasy of fulfilment he could give her in the heat of their marriage bed.

'You can say what you like about our marriage, about the past—but don't ever lie to me about that,' Zarek stated with icy precision. 'What there is between us in bed is special. I've never known anything like it. And I at least am not going to deny that.'

'I…'

Twice she opened her mouth to answer him, and both times her voice failed her completely. She didn't know how she could explain it to him anyway without ever using the three words that explained everything. The three words he didn't want to hear. She couldn't share his bed knowing that she loved him and that he had no feelings for her other than the powerful desire he had just stated so coldly.

Unable to use the words *I love you*, and finding it impossible to tell the man who had just demanded that she didn't lie to him, she gave up totally on speaking and could only shake her head in silent, desperate despair.

She knew just how he had interpreted her response by the way that his lips compressed hard and a revealing muscle tugged sharply in the right side of his jaw.

'All right, *glikia mou*, tonight you have it your way. Tonight we sleep alone. I will allow you the fact that we have been apart for two years—that we are like strangers again—for tonight at least. But I suggest that you take the night to think—to decide whether you want this marriage or not. Because after this, if we stay as husband and wife, then we stay in a real marriage, with everything that entails.'

A real marriage. The words were like a slap in the face, making her head spin nauseously. To her, a real marriage was one that was made in love and caring. A union of equals who each had given their heart to the other, But to Zarek, a *real* marriage was one that gave him the sexual satisfaction he sought, and the precious heir he had wanted all along.

And once he had that heir, just how long would that 'real' marriage last anyway?

'Zarek…'

But she was speaking to the back of her husband's head. He had turned away from her, wrenching open the door and stepping into the bedroom, striding away from her without even glancing back.

'Goodnight, Penny,' he said, cold and hard and totally distant. 'Sleep well.'

With a firm movement of his hand he slammed the door shut right in her face, giving it an extra push when closed as if needing to be sure.

What had he expected? Penny wondered bitterly. Did he think that she would be unable to cope with one night without him and that she would start to beg to be let back in? To beat on the door with her fists, begging and pleading.

Well, if he did then he was going to be bitterly disappointed. She knew when she had been dismissed and she had more pride than to go begging for him to change his mind, to open the door to her. Besides, this was exactly how she wanted things, wasn't it? To be free from the sexual enticement that she seemed to breathe in with the air that surrounded her long-lost husband and that had come straight back to torment her from the moment that he had walked into the house? She had meant what she said—that she didn't know him, and that she couldn't sleep with a man who didn't care about her.

At least that was what she told herself. So why was it suddenly so very hard to force her legs to walk away from the bedroom and take her towards the blue suite that she had already told Zarek was fully made up and ready for someone to sleep in? Why was she weakly tempted to do just what he seemed to have suspected might happen and crawl back to the closed door and…?

And what? Humiliate herself by begging to be let in? Reveal what a total fool she was where Zarek Michaelis was concerned and go to his bed, willing to take the little he might toss her way instead of holding out for the love she knew she needed? The love she deserved.

Even Argus had managed to sneak into Zarek's bedroom without risking rejection or coldness. And however jealous she might actually feel, she was not going to bring herself down to the level of the dog at his master's beck and call.

Marching into the blue room, she pulled off her clothes and dropped them on the floor. Then, naked because her night-clothes were in her original room, she slid into the bed, shivering faintly as the cool soft cotton chilled her skin.

It wasn't a cold night, she told herself. She would soon warm up. And she did, but even being warm and cosy in the soft, comfortable bed didn't mean that she could relax or that sleep came anywhere near as she lay restlessly awake, staring sightlessly into the darkness.

How was this possible? she couldn't help wondering. She had spent so many long nights lying awake until the early hours of the morning, feeling lost and alone and wishing, praying, that Zarek would come back from the depths of the dark sea that she had believed had swallowed him. If only he would be found alive, she had told herself, she would never complain again, never ask for more.

And now Zarek was back in her life. He was lying safe and sound just a few metres down the landing, probably fast asleep in the bed that he had said he had been dreaming about for so many months. Her every wish had come true and yet she felt so little of the happiness and the joy that she had told herself would lighten her heart if this night ever came.

The night she had dreamed of was here and yet she felt more lost and abandoned, more miserable and lonely than she had even been in all of the seven hundred and fifty other nights of Zarek's absence.

And the most terrible part of it was that deep in her heart she feared that there was far more—and worse—to come.

CHAPTER ELEVEN

PENNY HAD NO IDEA WHAT it was that woke her. She only knew that something had roused her from the shallow, restless sleep she eventually managed to find, startling her awake so that she sat bolt upright, shivering with a sense of shock.

'What? Who?'

When the sound came again, a harsh, choking cry, she knew at once that it was coming from the master bedroom just down the landing. The room where Zarek was sleeping.

Zarek.

His name was enough to push her out of bed, have her flinging open the door, running down the hallway.

'Zarek!'

The room was in darkness but the curtains had been left wide open and so the cold wash of moonlight lit up the bed where Zarek sprawled in a tangle of bedclothes. He was lying on his back, black hair wildly dishevelled against the fine white cotton, one arm flung up beside his head, the other stretched out across the bed. His bronzed chest was bare, the black hair that hazed it shadowy in the half-light, and the sheets were draped over the lower half of his powerful body, twisted and disturbed by his restless, fretful movements.

For a moment Penny froze in the doorway but as she watched

he stirred again, twisting from side to side and moaning in his sleep. It was all that she needed to push her forward, coming to the bed and dropping down onto the side of it. Reaching for his hands, she folded her own around them, stilling their agitated flailing as even in his sleep he felt her touch.

'Zarek,' she said softly. 'Darling—it's all right. I'm here.'

His deep, deep sigh seemed to come right from his soul, bringing tears to her eyes as she held on tight, willing him to know she was with him.

'You're not alone.'

Something in her voice got through to him. The lush black crescents of his eyelashes fluttered slightly then lifted slowly, his dark, unfocused gaze looking up into her watchful eyes.

'Penny? What…?'

His voice was rough and raw as if it came from a painfully sore throat.

'You were having a dream—a nightmare. I heard you call out.'

Zarek frowned for a moment, then closed his eyes again on another deep sigh.

'*Thee mou*, yes, I was—a dream… '

'Would it help to talk—can you tell me about it?'

She felt his shudder through the hands she held. Still keeping his eyes closed, he seemed to be reviewing the images his sleeping mind had projected, viewing them on the screen of his eyelids.

'The boat…' he began uncertainly.

'The *Troy*?'

But Zarek's response was a rough shake of his head.

'The small boat—the one the pirates came in.'

He'd been back in the boat where the pirates had taken him at gunpoint, Zarek recalled. In the hot, stinking, confined darkness of the small craft that pitched and tossed so violently on the waves that he feared that one of his captors' weapons might just fire by accident. All around him there had been panic and chaos, voices muttering savagely in a language he didn't understand, the wild arguments—obviously the debate over what they were going to do with him.

It had all been a form of wild confusion. He had no idea exactly in what order things had happened. He recalled the moment he had thought he saw an opening, the shouts getting louder, wilder. The explosive sound of a shot and the searing pain along his left temple. The icy cold that soaked into his clothes as he hit the water. And then the complete, the total blackness.

'Zarek?'

A voice called him back to reality. And it took a moment to realise that it was a voice here, now, in the present, and not the voice he could have sworn he had heard in the darkness, when he had drifted between waking and unconsciousness, never knowing where he was or what was happening.

'Penny?'

It was an effort to bring his mind back into focus. But the warm touch of her hands on his seemed like a lifeline to draw him back from the darkness. Slowly he opened his eyes, saw the pale shimmer of her skin in the moonlight.

'Penny! You must be freezing…'

'I'm O…'

But her protest was ruined by the small, uncontrolled shiver she gave. One that had him adjusting his position swiftly, pulling back the covers, flinging them open so that she could come into the bed beside him.

'But I—I've nothing on.'

'And neither have I. All the more reason for you to come and get warm. And it's not as if it's never happened before.'

Still she hesitated, and he thought she would actually refuse, but another involuntary shudder had her hurrying under the bedclothes, pulling them up around her. Her slender body was cold from the night air and she held herself stiff and straight, well away from him so they might have been miles apart rather than sharing the same bed. But in spite of that he knew a sense of relief. A real feeling of rightness that she should be there. The scent of her skin, her hair filled his nostrils, and the faint sound of her breathing helped him to relax.

'Do you want to talk about it?' Penny said quietly. Her eyes were fixed on the ceiling above her, deliberately not looking at him.

He opened his mouth to say no, it was over, done, he was fine…and found that instead he actually wanted to tell her about it. For the first time he wanted to share with someone the dark places that his mind could take him. To let out the memories that haunted his nights, disturbed his sleep, even when he hadn't known who he was or where those images had come from.

If she had said anything, asked a question, made a comment, then he felt he would have dried up at once, unable to go on. But she simply lay there, silent and receptive, and as he talked to her he felt the slow but definite softening of her body, the easing of tight muscles, the adjustment of her position. In the end she had curved towards him, her face turned to his and so close on the pillows that he could feel the softness of her breath on his cheek.

'I thought it was the end,' he said, and now he was the one staring up at the ceiling, eyes wide so that he didn't see the images of the black, black night, the empty, dark sea, even in his mind. But he felt the shiver that shook Penny's body and knew she was imagining it too.

'When you come close to death, you start to think about

what really matters and what doesn't. I realised then that
there was plenty in my life that I could let go of.'

Weird how a silence could be more encouraging than any
words. How even just the slight hitch in the smoothness of her
breathing could tell him she was still listening.

'Ambition, wealth, success wouldn't have held much value
then and there,' he said as if she had actually asked the
question. 'Even Odysseus Shipping could have crumbled and
it would have just been a challenge to start all over again.'

Beside him in the darkness, Penny stirred and he almost felt
her gaze on his shadowed face as she drew in another soft breath.

'And what does matter?' she whispered.

She had broken the silence, and she was so near... He
couldn't stay where he was and not touch her. Turning onto his
side so that he was facing her, he reached out to pull her close,
feeling her instinctive resistance, the tightening of every muscle.

'Relax, just let me hold you. Nothing else—I swear.'

He could almost hear the battle in her mind. But in the same
moments he felt again the softening of her body, the way she
inched forward until she was fitted against his side, and he
knew in that moment that nothing had ever before felt so
right. Folding his arms round her, he rested his head against
her hair and tried to answer her question.

'Loyalty, trust...'

None of the words seemed right. None of them fitted.

'At a time like that you wonder just who would care if you
didn't come back. Who would be waiting when you come...
home.'

Home. That word resonated so hard in his thoughts that it
stopped his speech. He had to wait, to let it sink in, absorb it.

'I felt alone,' he finally managed.

Beside him he heard Penny's breathing slow, deepen. The

warmth of the bed and the lateness of the hour were getting to her and he could sense her drifting. But just for a moment she stirred briefly, and he felt her eyelids flutter open against his throat.

'I would have...' she managed before sleep claimed her and she drifted into silence.

Would have? Zarek echoed in his thoughts. Would have cared? Would have waited?

Would she still have been here if the legal problems in finalising the declaration of his death hadn't kept her on Ithaca?

Of course I would have cared! The words she had flung at him earlier came back to him now, seemingly in response to the question, but not actually answering it in the end. *And not just 'cared' in the past but still care now! I might not want to be married to you any more, but I sure as hell would never, ever have wished you* dead!'

And that was when he knew there was one thing he hadn't been able to tell her. One thing that perhaps he could never tell her.

In the pirates' boat and then again in the dark, dark hours in the water. When he had drifted in and out of consciousness, there had been one thought that had always been there. The thought of this woman—his wife—and the difference she had made to his life. When he had thought that it would be easier to give up and just drift, let go, the thought of the way they had parted had somehow kept him from going under, made him hold on.

He had thought of Penny even when he hadn't known who she was. With his memory scrambled, and nothing of his life, this island—not even Odysseus Shipping—anywhere in his thoughts, she had come to him in his dreams when he didn't even know her name. It was the need to find out who she was that had kept him hunting for the truth.

He had wanted to come back to her. He had thought that then he would find what he was searching for.

It seemed impossible that in all the time he had spent away, even when he hadn't known who he was, he had dreamed of coming home—wherever 'home' might be. He had thought that when that happened his life would be changed. Complete. It would have the meaning that seemed so lacking while he was lost and wandering. He would finally know just who he was and where his place in life belonged.

'Belonged—hah!'

His low laugh was a sound of harsh cynicism, dark and rough, and it echoed round the silent stillness of the room in the empty house.

Empty all but for the woman curled up next to him in the bed asleep. The woman who had turned his life upside down from the moment he had first set eyes on her and who seemed determined to drive him out of his mind before he was very much older.

He was already part way there as it was. Half out of his head with wanting her and yet not knowing whether their marriage had a chance of surviving. When he had first come back to himself after long months of not even knowing who he was or where he lived, she had been the first person he had set himself to find out about. The wife he had left behind and who had now spent two years without him.

But that was before everything had come back to him. And what he had finally recalled, when put together with what he had heard, had left him determined to wait and watch.

That was when he had heard her state openly that she wanted him declared dead so that she could move on with her life. And when she had realised that her husband was in the room…

'Gammoto!'

Zarek's fist clenched tight as he recalled the way that Penny—that *his wife*—had looked at him in the moment that he had walked back into her life after two years' absence. Two years in which she hadn't known if he was alive or dead—and hadn't cared too much, if the way she had looked was anything to go by. Her whole face had frozen up, her eyes looking dead and emotionless, and she could barely get his name out when she spoke.

And since then she had played hot and cold depending on what suited her and the situation in which she found herself.

Or had she?

His hand twisted in the sheet that covered him, crushing the fine fabric ruinously as he recalled the way that the cool and distant woman who had offered him a sandwich and a coffee as if he had just come back home after a busy day at the office had suddenly turned into the passionate, fiery creature who had heated his bed and delighted his senses in the days, months, after their marriage. And then just as quickly turned back into the remote, unapproachable iceberg with the feeble excuse that she no longer knew him well enough.

And yet she was also the woman who had heard him cry out in the night and had come running so fast that she hadn't even stopped to put on any clothing.

He knew which woman he had wanted to come back to—but which was the real Penny? And had he ever seen her?

Dawn had barely broken but Zarek gave up any further pretence of trying to sleep. Moving carefully so as not to disturb the woman sleeping beside him, he slid out of bed and walked across to the window to stare out at the restless surface of the sea. The waves reflected his mood, looking edgy and agitated, swirling deep currents over the pebbled beach and lashing against the rocks on the shore.

This was where he belonged, where he lived. But home…?

A low plaintive whine broke into his angry thoughts and a cold black nose was pushed into the palm of his left hand where it hung at his side. Glancing down at the big black and white shape of Argus, Zarek smiled ruefully and ruffled the fur at the back of the big dog's neck.

'Had enough of being inside, hmm?' he asked softly. 'I know—you're desperate for a walk.'

And exercise might just help clear his own head. A run along the stony shore, drawing the ozone scented air into his lungs, pushing his body hard, driving himself until the sweat was dripping into his eyes, until he was too tired to think, too exhausted to care about the nagging ache that just lying with her—being with her anywhere—always created in his body.

Looking at her now, at the way she lay curled under the covers, her dark hair splayed across the pillows, her face relaxed, he was so strongly tempted to slide back into the bed and gather her close to him. To haul her up against him, and kiss her until they were both delirious with need just as he had wanted to do last night.

Then he had wanted to kiss the lying words 'I don't want it. I don't want you,' from her mouth and crush them back down her throat. And then he would have taken her to the bed—to their bed, their marriage bed—and made love to her until every last thought of 'not knowing' him was driven from her mind.

And he still wanted to do just that. Wanted it so much. All that was feminine in her called to every masculine sense in his own body, making him harden until he burned with need, ached with the frustration of holding it in check. But he was going to hold back if it killed him. He had been caught that way before, in the early days of their marriage. He'd rushed her into bed without taking time to find out who she really was and what she truly wanted. And they had ended up at the opposite sides of a wide, gaping chasm as a result.

A chasm that his dreams had told him was still there. Perhaps even wider than ever.

'I might not want to be married to you any more...'

Argus whined again and Zarek dragged his thoughts back to the present, opening the wardrobe to find something comfortable to run in. And once more his mind came to a sudden and jolting stop as he considered the packed interior of the cupboard.

She had kept all his clothes. Every item that he had left behind. They had all been carefully folded and replaced as if he had just set out for a simple business trip and was expected home at any minute. Would a woman who never wanted to see her husband again do anything like that?

The question nagged at him as he dressed. It burned in his thoughts as he pounded along the stony beach, Argus running ecstatically beside him. It was still there, still troubling him when he finally admitted that he could run no more and made his way back to the house, to shower in another bedroom so as not to wake Penny if she was still asleep, change into the clothes he had brought from the bedroom earlier.

And still he couldn't find any answer to the confusion of his thoughts.

He had to find some work to do. Work would distract him and focus his mind on other things. Work had always been his salvation in the past when he needed a distraction from the speed with which his marriage had gone to rack and ruin. The total change in the woman he had married.

His private office appeared just the same as when he had left it, with nothing touched, nothing moved. The computer and every other piece of equipment was in exactly the same place, unchanged. It had been kept clean and dusted so that again he had the unnerving feeling that it was as if he had just walked back in after being away for a day or so.

But it was when he unlocked one of the drawers and pulled it open that he found the first evidence of change, the first sign that someone had been in the office in his absence and had used the desk for anything more than just sitting at.

'What the…?'

Pulling the folder of papers from the drawer, Zarek opened it and spread them out over the polished top of the desk, staring in disbelief as he moved them around with his fingertips.

'I don't believe it.'

There was no doubt whatsoever who had been busy with these documents. Everywhere was the evidence of Penny's handwriting, easily recognisable even after all this time. But it seemed impossible that his wife would have anything to do with these…

And that was not the only puzzle. Once more he sorted through the papers before him, studying each one closely. There was something not quite right here. Something that didn't fully make sense. So many of the documents had been corrected, changed, with alterations made and then erased again, new ideas added all the time. And yet she could have handed over the first set and it would have been fine.

The sound of footsteps on the stairs alerted him. The study door was partly open as Penny came slowly down the wide curving staircase. He saw how she noticed the way it was standing ajar and paused, hesitating noticeably.

So if he said hello—spoke at all—would that encourage her or would it simply send her running again, heading back up the stairs or along the hallway into the big empty kitchen, away from him? He didn't have time to consider the question for long before she gave the door an uncertain push and appeared in the doorway.

'*Kalimera.*'

He kept his greeting cool and indifferent with an effort. It was impossible, unbelievable, but somehow it almost seemed as if the short time they had spent apart had actually been longer than the months they had been separated before yesterday. It was as if he was looking at her afresh, with brand-new eyes, and seeing her more clearly than ever before.

Seeing the changes he had not fully noticed in all the hours they had been together on the day before.

When he had met her she had been so young. Barely twenty-two, just a girl, working in her first job. Her face still had the softness, the faint roundness of youth, and her tall, slender figure had been almost boyish in its narrow shape. She had grown up in the past two years, her face thinning, her features refining so that she had the most devastating high, slanting cheekbones under her beautiful almond-shaped blue eyes. And her body had filled out slightly, adding gentle curves to an almost too-slender shape so that now she was no longer a girl but all woman, a woman just coming into her fully feminine prime and fulfilling all the stunning promise of her youth.

Dear heaven, but she even made the well-worn pink tee shirt and faded, shrunken jeans she wore look fantastic. No silken designer gown or elegant evening dress could look any better or flatter that glorious body any more. Briefly Zarek had to wonder if she had simply pulled on the nearest things to hand or whether the slightly shabby clothing had been chosen to distract him, disguise the sensual appeal of her body. If that was the case then she had failed dramatically. The way that the shrunken top clung to the curves of her breasts and narrow ribcage, riding up to reveal an inch or two of smooth golden skin, was pure temptation. And the denim, washed soft by repeated laundering, clung to her hips and thighs in a way that made his pulse pound, his body tightening in instant response.

'Good morning.'

Her response was cooler even than his own. And she was back to being the ice maiden again, with her face frozen into a distant mask, those blue eyes seeming to look straight through him without a flicker of emotion.

'It's a beautiful day.'

Oh, this was ridiculous, Penny told herself. They were speaking to each other as if they were near strangers. And yet she had fallen asleep, naked, in his arms.

And woken to find him gone.

'Did you get any sleep in the end?' Oh, how formally conventional could she get?

'No.'

Zarek's response brought her up short. Such honesty was the last thing she had been expecting. What she had anticipated was that the conversation was going to carry on in the way it had started, with the pair of them dancing round the reality of their situation, resorting instead to meaningless inanities.

No man should have the right to look so good this early in the morning, she thought, taking in the loose navy shirt he wore with black denim jeans, the way that his hair, still damp from the shower, curled slightly around his ears and at the nape of his neck as it began to dry in the heat. Particularly not after a sleepless night. Lying awake herself, she had heard him get up at a ridiculous hour and go downstairs, Argus pattering happily behind him.

When the front door had opened she had gone to her own bedroom window and looked out to see him setting off towards the shore, dressed only in black running shorts and a pair of battered trainers. The rising sun had gilded the jet-black hair, the olive skin of his long back, the powerful shoulders, and the lean, muscled length of his legs. All of which had featured in the heated, erotic dreams that had burned into her brain through the little sleep she had had. She had watched him hungrily as he ran down the narrow path, unable to drag her eyes away. Her throat had been dry and tight with longing; the memory of the feel of that skin under her fingers, the musky male scent of it in her nostrils made her heart clench with longing.

The long lonely hours at the beginning of night had brought home to her just how much she had lost without Zarek in her life. The physical hunger was like the bite of acid deep in her stomach, eating away at her and at her resolution to hold herself apart from him, the determination that she needed emotional love before she could give into the fury of sexual need that he awoke in her. Then when she'd slipped into his bed the feeling that had tugged at her heart had been one of perfect rightness, a sense of coming home. She had known then that if he had tried to seduce her she wouldn't have been able to resist it. She wouldn't even have tried.

But he hadn't touched her. Instead he had been intimate with her in a very different way, by opening up to her as she had never expected he would. And she had drifted asleep held close in his arms.

'But I'm glad that you made up for your earlier restlessness,' Zarek told her. 'I heard you pacing around your room. It seems that Argus was the only one who slept all night.'

He dropped a hand onto the big dog's head and rubbed it softly and, as before, Argus pushed himself against the caressing touch, his eyes closing in ecstasy. Once again Penny thought that she knew exactly how he felt, and the sight of those long, bronzed fingers ruffling the thick black and white fur had her compressing her lips tightly against the whimper of need that almost escaped her.

The thought of him lying awake listening to her prowling restlessly round her bedroom was tying her stomach into tight painful knots. Had he guessed at the yearning hunger that had kept her awake, the need that had made it impossible even to lie still in her bed? Penny's heart kicked up a gear at the thought, her pulse beating erratically at her temples and the base of her throat.

'Have you had any breakfast?'

Back on the conventionally polite track once again, she acknowledged. It was safer that way. Far less dangerous than trying any other sort of conversation that might let her foolish tongue betray her terribly.

'Should I get you something—that is unless the staff are back today? No?' she questioned as Zarek shook his dark head.

'No. I told them I would let them know when to come back. Until then they are all on paid leave.'

'So—so we're alone?' Her apprehension at the thought showed in the way that her voice quavered on the last word.

'We're alone and there is no need for this incessant desire to feed me. You don't have to keep demonstrating that you have benefited from the cookery lessons you've taken. I'm much more interested in the other skills that you seem to have acquired.'

'What other skills exactly?'

For a shocking moment, with her own thoughts still clouded by sensual hunger, she thought he actually meant some sort of skills in the bedroom and felt the hot blood rush into her cheeks as a result. But just in time she saw the plans he had in his hands and caught back the hasty words that rushed to her tongue.

'It was you who worked on these? The plans for the *Calypso*?'

She couldn't tell just what his tone meant, but there was no point in denying the truth when it was so obviously there in her handwriting, her notes.

'Yes… Yes, I worked on them.'

His response was the last thing she expected. He actually laughed. Not in mockery or even real amusement. It was a laugh of disbelief and he shook his head in obvious bemusement at the same time.

'You did all this?'

'I said I did.'

'No need to get so defensive, *glikia mou*. I'm amazed— and impressed. I never knew you had such talent or the knowledge to use it. I'm sure that you didn't when I left.'

'I listened to you, and then I studied—two years is a long time.'

'So it seems. You continue to surprise me. So what else will I discover that I never knew about my wife? What else did you learn while I wasn't here?'

When he smiled at her like that she found it impossible to think of anything else. When his mouth softened and curved, and his eyes warmed in genuine delight, there was only one thought that formed inside her head, one feeling that she recognised at all. It was the lesson she had learned with the most pain and difficulty from the day that Zarek had walked out of the house and set out for the *Troy*. The one that had been reinforced with every hour he had been absent and all the terrible days when she believed that he was dead. And it was a lesson that had been driven home again with dreadful brutality as she had lain alone last night, trying desperately to sleep and fearing that no rest would ever come.

The one thing the past two years had taught her was that

life without Zarek in it was not *living*. It was nothing more than existing, dragging herself through the days without meaning, without hope, without joy. Loving Zarek was what gave her life its purpose, its significance, its delight. She could go through her days without him and even make a reasonable go of things. She'd done that, hadn't she? She had learned new skills, discovered strengths she'd never known she had, and she had thought that she was managing well. But he had only to walk back into her life, to be part of her life once again for—what, was it really not quite twenty-four hours?—and everything became so much brighter, the world so much better simply because he was in it.

She loved him totally and completely. He was the essence of her world, the breath in her lungs, the sun coming up in the morning. And last night, lying lost and alone without him, she had learned the most painful, most powerful lesson of all.

It didn't matter whether Zarek loved her or not. He wanted her and that was enough. She wouldn't ask for anything more. She couldn't ask for it, for fear that he would tell her what she already knew deep down was the darkest truth. That he had nothing to give her but his passion.

But if she could entice him back into her bed then perhaps she could keep him with her at least.

'Penny?' Zarek's rough—voiced prompting told her that she had been standing there for too long without speaking. 'What else is there?'

'What else is there?' she echoed, looking into his face and knowing there was only one answer. If his passion was all he felt for her, all he would give her, then it would be enough. She had enough love for the both of them and she shared that blazing, burning physical passion too. Without it life was just not worth living but with it she had Zarek and the wonderful, glorious excitement they could create between them.

She was not going to give up on that very easily.

'What else? Well, to my mind there's only one thing worth bothering about. And that is—no…'

She caught herself up deliberately, tilted her head slightly to one side as she gazed deep into the darkness of his eyes. Slowly she slid her tongue out and slicked it across her bottom lip, smiling faintly as she watched his dark eyes drop down to follow the small movement.

'No, I don't think I'll tell you—I'll show you.'

Leaning forward, she pressed her mouth to Zarek's, feeling the sudden tiny start of shock, the faint gasp of his breath in between his lips.

'Show you exactly what I've learned since you were last here.'

And taking the two small steps it needed to be close up against the hard warmth of his lean body, she pressed herself to him, moulding her frame to his as she linked her arms around his neck, tangled her fingers in the dark slippery silk of his hair, and drew his head down to her so that she could deepen the embrace.

'I've learned that *this* is the only thing that matters.'

CHAPTER TWELVE

I've learned that this is the only thing that matters.

There was something in that sentence that jarred, sticking a mental knife in just when Zarek least expected—or wanted—it. But he didn't have time or the inclination to stop and consider just what it was that nagged at him. Penny's lips were on his, the taste of her filling his mouth. The sweet scent of her body was all around him, the warmth of her skin against his.

This was what he'd longed for since his memory had come back. Before that, he had remembered her in his subconscious, in heated, yearning flashes, in hot, erotic dreams that had him tossing and turning through the night, awakening soaked in sweat, with his heart racing as if he had run the race of his life.

And the worst part of waking had been the hunger, the craving that had filled his sleep and that still lingered long after he had woken, even after he had drenched himself in the coldest shower possible. In his sleep he had reached out to the warm and willing woman that aroused his senses, only to find that when he opened his eyes there was no one there.

That was not going to happen this time.

This time the woman he remembered was safely in his arms, her mouth taking his, the swell of her breasts pressed up against his chest. This time was no dream from which he had any fear of waking. It was real, it was hot, it was the fulfilment of his sensual fantasises and he was going to take full advantage of it.

In fact it was more than he had ever dreamed of. Because in those dreams, the woman he now knew as his wife had been warm and willing, but a little hesitant, almost softly shy as she responded to his touch, his kiss. She had been responsive but not proactive. He had been the one to initiate intimacy while she had been the giver, opening softly to him, welcoming him, but not taking the initiative.

The woman in his arms now was all forwardness and enticement, her actions coming close to demand. Her mouth took his with hunger, her tongue dancing with his in a wild, erotic provocation. Her rounded hips pressed against his hot and aching sex, making him groan aloud in barely controlled need in the same moments that her fingers tugged at the buttons on his shirt, ripping them open as if she couldn't wait to touch and taste his burning flesh. The moist pressure of her lips against his hardened nipple made him jolt sharply as if a sudden bolt of electricity had shot right through him.

'*Glikia mou…*' The words sounded rough and raw, coming from a throat that was tight with the tension of need. 'Not so fast. This has been a long time coming and we have all the time in the world. Slow down.'

She didn't want to slow down, Penny told herself. She didn't want to give him, or herself, any time to think. They might have all the time in the world, but only if she could show him that they were meant to be together. If she could convince him that she was the woman he needed, the woman he couldn't live without.

And the way to do that was through the blazing passion

that had always fired between them in the past. A hunger so hot she had felt it might almost melt her bones in its furnace, bringing her to her knees before it. In the past, in their marriage bed, she had always been a little shy, always allowed him to take the lead, to be the seducer and she the seduced. But that had been when she had believed that their marriage would have time and space in which to grow, and deepen. Time that she had thought she had lost completely when he had gone missing. Time she no longer had now that he was home.

And so she pressed herself even closer up against him, almost pushing him backwards until he was hard up against the wall, his shirt ripped from his back, the golden planes of his chest exposed to the hungry attentions of her mouth and tongue.

'I don't want to slow down,' she muttered, sighing, against his skin, inhaling the clean musky scent of him that sent her senses spiralling as if under the influence of some potent, intoxicating drug. 'I want you now.'

'And I…' Zarek managed before she closed his mouth again with hers, letting her hands take over from her lips, touching, stroking, teasing. She even let her nails score a delicate path down to his waist, making him jerk in wild, uncontrolled response.

'*Eisai o sizigos mou.*'

From somewhere she dragged up one of the phrases in Greek that he had taught her.

'You are my husband…you—*ise o adras mou*—you are my man. And I want my man—I want him now.'

'*Gamoto!*'

Zarek's rough curse was forced out of him as she deliberately let her wandering hands slide down to where the heat and power of his erection strained against the zip on his trousers, his choking moan making her smile with a new and very welcome sense of the power she had over him.

But as she fumbled with the buckle on his belt, tugging it free with a sense of impatience, Zarek suddenly changed the mood, the balance of the moment. No longer content to be the one who was under sensual assault, he shifted, changed position and became the one who was in control. Capturing her hands, her arms, he lifted her bodily from the floor and carried her across the room to where the long, low couch stood before the empty fireplace.

'And I want my woman,' he muttered roughly, laying her down on the cushions and coming down beside her before she even had time to snatch in a much-needed, hungry breath.

He was much more efficient at dealing with her clothes than she had been with his and it was only moments before the tee shirt and jeans were tossed aside, her underwear following them. His own trousers were dropped to the floor as Zarek came over her naked, hungry body, crushing her into the yielding cushions with the force of his weight and strength.

His skin was hot against hers, his hands rousing her to even greater heights of hunger, and she urged him on with moaning, hungry cries that seemed to drive him to the edge of distraction. When she combined them with insistent, urgent, provocative caresses that had him almost snarling her name in a wild blend of need and encouragement, he lost control completely, pushing her legs wide apart with the forceful pressure of one knee and driving himself into her body with barely a heartbeat's pause.

But Penny hadn't wanted any pause. This wonderful, this total possession was all she had wanted and she arched herself against him with a cry of delight, raising her hips to meet him, to take him fully into her where she had wanted him so long and where she had feared she would never ever feel him again.

'Zarek—yes!'

With her lips and her hands she encouraged him in the storm of sensual passion that had them both in its grip, fingers closing over the strength of his shoulders, digging into the tight hard muscles she found there, urging him on. Above her she saw his face, set in the hard, determined lines of passion, his eyes glazed with need, a sharp line of colour etched along his carved cheekbones.

'Oh, Zarek—yes. My man—my husband and my—'

Somehow still retaining the tiniest bit of rational thought, but only just in time, she caught back the betraying final word my *love*. But even if she had let it escape, she doubted if he would have heard it. And a moment later she too was incapable of speech, of thought. She was flying, soaring, reaching for the sun, the stars, losing herself completely in the wonder of the fulfilment she had hungered for for so long.

The explosion of ecstasy was so powerful that she would have sworn she actually lost consciousness for a moment or two, holding onto Zarek by pure instinct, welcoming his powerful climax into her yielding body for as long as she possibly could. Only when he collapsed against her with a cry of satisfaction did she allow herself to let go, to fall back against the couch and let herself float on the heated golden waves of the aftermath of total pleasure.

She had no idea how long she lay there, drifting in and out of consciousness. It was only when some small sense of reality began to creep back into her world that she felt Zarek sigh and lift his head. A moment later he had rolled away from her, lying on his back beside her. Drawing in his breath in a rough, uneven sound, he reached up and raked both hands roughly through his hair, cursing in dark Greek phrases as he did so.

'Zarek?' It was all that she could manage but a rush of

concern forced its way through the glowing haze that still throbbed inside her head. 'What…?'

He moved again, stirring restlessly at her side.

'We didn't use protection.'

If it was possible to freeze while her breath was still ragged and uneven, her chest still heaving, and her heart racing as if she had run the fastest marathon ever, then Penny froze. At least her thoughts did, her brain seeming to come to a complete halt as if under the effects of a powerful punch to her jaw. And in spite of the warmth of the morning, the sun that was streaming through the window, she suddenly felt as if she were sheathed in ice from head to toe, shivering violently as a result.

But it was the terrible sense of shock and horror that was making her tremble. The cold that was creeping through her body was created by a sense of horror and disbelief rather than any effect of the weather.

'What…?'

She tried to ask a question but it seemed to evaporate on her tongue, leaving her mouth opening and closing until she felt she must look like a stranded fish, gasping for breath.

'What did you say?' she managed at last, but her voice was little more than a croak and she could barely hear the words herself.

Zarek caught them though and he turned his dark head to glance at her briefly, coldly. Then almost immediately he looked away again, throwing his head back on the cushions as he stared up at the ceiling.

'I think you heard me,' he drawled coldly. 'But just to make certain—I realised that we didn't use any protection. I wasn't expecting…unless you're still on the pill?'

'No, I'm not.'

It was as she said the words that the full implications of what she had said hit home. Suddenly finding that she could move, she flung herself upright on the settee, twisted round to stare at him.

'No, I'm not!'

'Then I think we could be in trouble here.'

A cynically mocking sideways glance from those dark, dark eyes challenged her, draining all the earlier heat from her body from her and leaving her with a devastating sensation of being totally bloodless, any strength fleeing from every nerve in the space of a shaken, wretched heartbeat. She knew that her skin must have lost all colour and that her own eyes were wide and staring, their blue colour probably clouded with the brutal sense of shock and disbelief.

Zarek by contrast looked totally relaxed and at his ease. Totally unconcerned by his nudity, his long body stretched out full length on the couch, narrow feet resting on the padded arm at the far end. His hands were linked behind his neck, supporting his head, heavy lids dropping down to conceal his brilliant jet eyes from her. Lying like this, he looked like nothing so much as a sleepy, sexually replete jungle cat relaxing in the sunshine. But Penny knew only too well that the appearance was deceptive. Make the wrong move—or say the wrong thing—and the contented pussycat would turn instantly into a powerful, predatory tiger hunting down his prey and determined to deliver a brutal retribution for the disturbing of his rest.

Just for a moment those hooded lids lifted, flashed one quick, coldly assessing glance in her direction...

'One thing's for sure, there's no way you'll be able to use that desertion excuse for divorce now,' Zarek continued, the words practically a darkly dangerous purr. 'The two-year separation you accused me of yesterday is well and truly over.'

She'd thought she'd been distressed enough yesterday. Thought that she was too afraid to go through with making love with Zarek when she felt she didn't know him well enough after his long absence and all she had learned about him in that time, to risk being intimate with him. Now she had given into the yearning hunger his touch awoke in her and look where it had led her.

Feeling suddenly very grubby and tainted, shamed and terribly used, Penny couldn't bear to stay beside him any longer. Pushing herself away from him with a force that carried her across the rug, to land uncomfortably in one of the big padded armchairs opposite, she curled up into a defensive bundle, wrapping her arms around herself to hold herself together, trying to stop the shaking that racked her body.

'That's what it was all about!'

She couldn't keep the horror from her voice or disguise the disgust she felt at the way she'd been treated.

'That's all it was—a way to keep me as your wife—trap me into sleeping with you so that you could… That was what this was about.'

'Not at all,' Zarek told her calmly, easing himself into an upright position. 'I wanted to remind you of what we had between us—but I should also point out to you that you were the one who started all this. You were the one who said that *"this is the only thing that matters"…*'

He echoed her words, her voice, with such devastating accuracy that Penny couldn't control a painful shudder of reaction at hearing what she had said. And hearing just how she had said it.

Had she really sounded so huskily seductive, so provocative? She had never dared to do anything like that in all the time they had been married. She had felt the passion, adored making love with Zarek, but she had never had the real confidence to show it or take the initiative. At the beginning it had all been too new and she had felt so shy with this amazing man who seemed, unbelievably, to want her so much. And then when she had discovered that he only wanted her to provide him with an heir, shock and pain had made her withdraw from him, their lovemaking never the same again. The thought that she might have lost him for ever had changed all that. It was no wonder that Zarek believed she was different.

'I thought that was what you wanted.'

'I'd be a fool to deny that.'

Zarek's laugh was shaken, rough-edged.

'But I'm not usually this irresponsible. This stupid.'

Irresponsible. Stupid. She had wanted to make love to the man who had her heart and he thought it had been *stupid*.

'Oh, don't worry about it.'

She tried for bravado, acting as if she didn't care. She even managed to sort of shrug it off.

'It doesn't matter.'

'Even if it means that you might end up pregnant?'

The question hit her like a slap in the face. She really hadn't even considered that, hadn't spared a thought for the fact that they were not using any contraception. Or if the idea had flashed through her mind then she had pushed it away again, the need that was driving her far too powerful for caution.

Now she had to consider it. And do more than consider it. Because the look on Zarek's face had turned her blood to ice. Was it possible that just when she had resolved that her future lay with him, no matter what, *he* had decided that a child and a future with her was the last thing he wanted?

'I don't want to talk about it.'

Not like this, not sitting here stark naked, totally exposed in all possible ways, physically, emotionally. Somehow she made herself face him, schooling her expression into a total blank, revealing nothing.

'I'd like my clothes, please.'

Was that cold stiff little voice really hers?

'Your servant, ma'am…' Zarek murmured cynically, strolling over to where her jeans and tee shirt lay on the floor. Snatching them up, he tossed them in her direction, not caring that they fell several inches short and landed in a crumpled heap at her feet. She grabbed for them and scrambled into them as quickly as she could, well aware of the fact that he was pulling on his own clothes with much less haste and more efficiency. That, combined with the fact that he only pulled his shirt on, leaving it unbuttoned, meant that he was dressed well before her, giving him an unfair advantage. But with her own clothes on she at least regained some degree of confidence, ready to face whatever came.

And Zarek barely gave her time to pull the pink tee shirt over her head before he spoke again.

'Penny—if you are pregnant…' he began and the sombre expression, the dark tone, seemed to tell their own story.

'Don't!'

It was a cry of distress and she had to fight with herself not to put her hands over her ears, knowing she didn't want to hear him pronounce her fate.

'Don't tell me you don't want…won't want a baby—'

'Don't want?' Zarek cut across her in obvious consternation. 'But it was you who never wanted a child. You said—'

'I know what I said—and I lied!'

That stopped him dead. His hands that had gone to the buttons on his shirt now fell away again, leaving it gaping open over the wide expanse of his chest. Penny could see the marks on his skin where her nails had caught him in the heat of their passion and she shivered in reaction to the realisation of just how out of control she had been.

'You lied?'

She didn't think that the muscles in his face could get any tighter, or his eyes darker and more distant. But she had come this far now. There was no going back.

'I lied when I said I didn't want a child. I did—I do. Just not…'

'Just not my child,' Zarek finished for her when her tongue stumbled, unable to get the words out.

There was something in his tone that meant she couldn't leave it like that, no matter what the consequences.

'Just not your heir!' she flashed at him and saw the way a frown snapped his black brows together in confusion.

'Not my heir—my child. But they are both the same thing.'

'No, they're not! Not at all! A child would be created out of love—the start of a family. Our family. But an heir—an heir to Odysseus Shipping—to keep Hermione, your stepbrothers, from getting their hands on the company—that's what you married me for, isn't it?'

'I married you—' Zarek began but Penny couldn't let him continue. She couldn't bear it if he lied to her now. If he tried to dodge the truth. Because that was what she could see in his face. That he was actually going to try to soften the blow and, while her heart twisted with longing to hear the more gentle words from him, she knew she couldn't let it happen. That only the truth would do.

'Tell me the truth, Zarek. Give me that at least. You never loved me when you married me. You wanted me in your bed. And you wanted an heir.'

The moments before he spoke seemed to last a lifetime.

And each one of them made her heart thud so painfully against her ribcage that she felt it was impossible to catch her breath, that she might actually pass out from the stress.

But then, slowly, and strangely almost sadly, Zarek nodded his dark head.

'Yes,' he responded harshly but so clearly that there could be no doubt as to exactly what he was saying. 'Yes, that's exactly why I married you.'

CHAPTER THIRTEEN

WELL, what had she expected? Penny asked herself. She had demanded the truth—had practically forced it out of him. So how could she complain when that truth tore her heart into pieces and left her bleeding and raw?

She didn't understand why it should hurt any more this time. After all, it was only what she had lived with before, what she had decided that she couldn't go on with any longer. But the trouble was that this time around she knew she couldn't make that decision all over again. She had already admitted to herself that she would have to put up with it. She had no other choice. She would take the little Zarek had to offer her and live with it. Because the two years without him had taught her that life without the man she loved in it was no life at all.

'Thank you,' she began, icy with control. But even as she drew in a breath to complete the sentence a sudden uproar from outside broke into what she was trying to say, drowning her voice and making it impossible to continue.

The first thing was the sound of cars. Lots of cars and motorbikes racing up to the gates at the end of the drive, screeching to a halt. Then doors slamming, feet on the stones, on the grass. A knock at the door loud and long and deafeningly persistent.

'Kyrie Michaelis—are you there? Is it true that you're home—that you're safe?'

'Just a few questions…'

'Can we have a word—an interview?'

And mingling with the demands, the questions, was Argus' low deep bark from behind the front door as he warned off the crowd who had suddenly descended on the house.

'Who is it?'

Startled, shocked, Penny could only stare round her in bewilderment, looking into Zarek's face for some explanation of what was happening.

'What's going on?'

But apart from a deep black frown that drew his brows together and the way he was shaking his head in disbelief, Zarek seemed to have no answer to give her. At least not one that could be heard above the pounding of fists on the door, the persistent, appalling, loud ringing of the doorbell.

Penny put her hands up to cover her ears, to try to drown out the battery of noise.

'What is it? What's happening?'

Unable to bear it a moment longer she dashed across to the window, pulling back a corner of the curtains to look outside.

'Penny—no!'

Zarek was right behind her, launching himself at her to grab hold of her arm, pull her away, drag her back into the middle of the room. But not before she had caught sight of what looked like a milling crowd of people outside. Men and women scrambling over each other to get near the door—or the window when they saw the curtains move. Pushing each other out of the way, elbowing them in the ribs, shoving them aside.

There were microphones and voice recorders and…

The flash of a couple of dozen or more camera bulbs made Penny jump in fright.

'What—?' she began, but as soon as she had started to speak she suddenly knew what was happening, realisation dawning in the same moment that Zarek swore darkly and confirmed what she suspected.

'The paparazzi, damn them. Someone has told them that I'm here and of course they couldn't miss out on a story like that. I can just see the headlines now—"Billionaire Returns from the Grave…"'

'And would that be so bad?'

Now that she knew what was happening, Penny was no longer quite so disturbed. Of course the press would be interested in Zarek's return. His every move had been of interest to the celebrity magazines, the social columns, before they had married and their wedding had been the event of the year with editors of glossy magazines offering small fortunes— more than small ones—for exclusive access to the event, private photographs, the whole 'whirlwind' romance story.

'You want to face them now?' Zarek questioned dryly, gesturing to their disordered clothes, the wild tangle of her hair.

And there was only one answer to that, Penny acknowledged, shuddering faintly at the thought. How could they face the press pack now, after what had just happened? How could they even consider an interview or photographs looking like this? And feeling even worse.

Twitching the curtain back again, she peeped out, then jumped back as an explosion of flashbulbs burst right in her face, or so it seemed, blinding her for a moment.

'Penny, get back! Look, it's me they want—I'll get rid of them. And then…'

The rest of what he was saying was drowned by another

storm of sound as Argus, held in check only by the door, doubled the intensity of his barking, throwing himself at the wood, roaring a challenge to all the intruders into his territory.

Zarek was gone before she could react or say anything and it was when he had left the room that Penny registered the way there had been an extra tension in his body, a raw edge to his voice. Something about his attitude brought thoughts of the night they had just spent together. The dream Zarek had had, and the memories that had shaken him so badly.

And those terrible words. 'I felt alone.'

As she watched she saw him open the door, saw the horde of reporters rush forward. And just for a split second, too brief for anyone in the crowd to notice, she saw him flinch, saw the betraying gesture of his hand lifted to fret at the scar that she had seen so many times before and knew what it meant.

Alone.

Well, she wasn't going to stand here and just watch through the window, Penny told herself. She couldn't let him go through this on his own, with no one at his side. Pushing rough hands through her hair in a vain attempt to restore it to some sort of order and straightening her clothing as best she could, she hurried after her husband.

Zarek cursed the arrival of the paparazzi. It was just what he did not need right now. What he needed was time and peace and quiet in which to get to the bottom of just what was going through Penny's mind and, hopefully, to see just where everything had started to go wrong.

Because it had gone wrong. And gone far further than he had ever dreamed.

'Kyrie Michaelis! A word!'

'Zarek—just a question—or two…'

Another explosion of flashbulbs almost blinded him,

making him pause on the threshold to blink away the coloured blotches that had formed in his eyes so that he couldn't see where he was going. Experience of being in a situation like this in the past had taught him that the only thing to do was to paint a smile on your face and keep a pleasant tone on your tongue. Anything else would be taken as an indication of a story he was trying to hide. A bigger story than the one they thought they were covering. And if they didn't find it then they would make one up. But he had had two years without this sort of exposure and somehow he seemed to have lost the knack of switching on the public image as soon as it was needed.

'What happened to you? Where have you been?'

The problem was that his mind was not fully on the situation outside the villa. His thoughts were inside the house, with Penny, seeing the look on her face, hearing the ice cold tone of her voice.

You wanted me in your bed. And you wanted an heir.

The words she had used rang inside his head, almost but not quite drowning out the persistent questions from the crowd of reporters in front of him. Somehow he supplied some answers. He knew he said Malta and amnesia and when they spotted the scar at his temple the flashbulbs went off with renewed fury. But all the time it was Penny's words, Penny's voice that nagged at his thoughts.

I lied when I said I didn't want a child. I did—I do.

Just not your heir.

'Mr Michaelis, is it true that you will now be getting a divorce?'

'What?'

That question got through all the other confusion that was buzzing in his mind. That question couldn't be answered off the top of his head, without thought. He didn't even know why they had asked it.

'We heard that you will now be getting a divorce.'

'Where did that come from?' As if he didn't know. Hermione—or Jason—was stirring up trouble again. But just the way he felt hearing the words told him what he had to do. What mattered.

But first he had to get rid of the paparazzi.

'Your stepmother told us—so is it true?' the reporter persisted.

'Is it true?' Zarek echoed coldly, dark eyes raking over the crowd in contempt. 'What do you think? Would I want to change the way things are when I have just come home to be with the woman I love?'

'But, Mr Michaelis—'

'Enough!'

He was tempted to let go of Argus' collar and let the dog clear the driveway of the reporters. But right now he had more important matters on his mind. He needed to get back into the house and talk to Penny.

'No more questions—no more photographs.'

He was moving back towards the door, taking the dog with him. A few more questions were thrown his way, a few more cameras flashed, but most of the crowd seemed to realise that they were not going to get any more out of him and already they were packing up their equipment, melting away.

Zarek didn't care what they did. He didn't pause, didn't look back until he was in the house. At one moment he glanced towards the door and saw Penny standing there, in the hallway, obviously having heard everything that had been said.

Good. The sight gave him some satisfaction. At least he would have one thing less to explain.

It was when her eyes connected with his and he saw the blank, closed-off expression in them that he felt an uncomfortable jolt. He saw her blue eyes flash just once in open defiance and anger before she turned and walked away. There was no warmth in her face, no hint of a smile. So perhaps she hadn't heard.

Closing the door firmly on the departing crowd, he released Argus and went looking for her.

'Penny—where are you?'

Penny was reluctant to answer his call. All she wanted to do was to go upstairs, pack and get out of the house as soon as possible. She didn't want to see Zarek's face ever again. But even she couldn't decide if it was because she was so furious at him for what he had done or because it would hurt so desperately to look into his eyes and know once and for all just how ruthless and uncaring he was. How little he cared for her.

She had kept out of sight behind the half-closed door so no one had seen her there. But she had seen everything that happened. Heard every word.

Heard every word that had fallen from Zarek's lying, cruel lips. The lips that such a short time before had kissed her into a delirium of delight and that now had coldly and callously dropped the most blatant lie into the waiting ears of the reporters, and no doubt into tomorrow's gossip column reports.

And she'd heard that appalling question.

'Mr Michaelis, is it true that you will now be getting a divorce?'

For a moment the world had swung round her, blurring dangerously until she felt desperately nauseous. She had reached out to clutch at the door, holding onto its much-needed support, forcing herself to breathe slowly and deeply until her head cleared. Then she had made herself look again.

And that was when Zarek had opened his mouth and told the most appalling lie she had ever heard him speak.

Or, correction, the first lie she had ever heard him speak.

Because no matter what else Zarek might have done he had never been a liar.

'Would I want to change the way things are,' he had said, 'when I have just come home to be with the woman I love?'

'Penny!'

He wasn't going to let her get away. At least not until she had faced him.

'Penny, where are you?'

Reluctantly Penny appeared in the doorway, her whole body taut, her head held stiffly upright. Once again, she tried the technique of not quite focusing her gaze so that she didn't have to look him straight in the face. There was the sound like a thousand angry bees buzzing inside her head and she couldn't concentrate on anything.

All she could think of was the way that Zarek had made love to her— Oh, dear God, no—he hadn't made love to her! He'd had sex with her, cold-blooded deliberate sex, with one intention only. That of making sure that she couldn't divorce him and—and maybe even to leave her pregnant as he had always wanted. And then—then… Her brain felt as if it would explode at just the thought of it—

Then he had had the nerve to declare to the reporters outside that he had come home to the woman he loved. The woman he *loved*. Zarek had never loved her. He had just told her so to her face.

Vaguely she became aware that Zarek was coming towards her, dark triumph in his eyes. He even smiled at her as he came close.

And she completely lost control of her temper.

'How dare you!' she exploded, stopping him dead. He hadn't expected her to come out fighting. It was written all over his face.

'How dare I what?' Zarek asked. 'Penny—what…?'

'Don't you, "Penny—what?" me! I know what was going on. I saw you, heard you… I heard you lie.'

'No, I—'

'Yes!'

She actually stamped her foot in rage, making Argus come running in from the kitchen to see what was happening.

'How dare you claim to love me in front of those reporters?'

'I didn't *claim*—I did not do it for that. Why would I?'

He actually reached out to her, almost took hold of her fingers, but she flung up her arms in a gesture of rejection, knocking his hand away.

'Because we both know that…know that…'

Her breath caught in her throat making her gasp out loud, unable to go on.

'Know what, Penny?' Zarek asked and she couldn't make out just what his tone was putting into the words.

'That you only married me because you wanted to found a Michaelis dynasty and have an heir to leave Odysseus Shipping to.'

She could only be grateful that he had stopped coming closer to her now. He had frozen completely, standing stock-still, just a metre or so away from her. But for all that the distance they were apart was so small everything about him, the expression in his eyes, the way he held his long lean body so stiffly taut, made her feel as if a huge gaping chasm had opened up between them. One so big that it would be totally impossible ever to bridge it.

'And you think that is the only reason why I married you?' The question might have been formed in ice, the words were so cold and stiff.

'I know it!' Penny cried. 'Oh—you fancied me—you made

that obvious of course! You couldn't keep your hands off me. Which must have made it all the easier for you.'

'You think?'

'I know. After all, there wasn't much else going for me. I only have to think of that carved bed head to know—'

'I had a carving made,' Zarek interrupted, 'Just for you.'

'Oh, yes.'

She couldn't erase the bitterness from her tone.

'Oh, yes—the mouse. The damn *mouse*.'

But Zarek was shaking his head, sending his dark hair flying over his forehead.

'But not just any mouse.'

'Oh, how can you say that? A mouse is a mouse—small, creeping, nervous… Insignificant.'

'But not this one. Come here…'

Penny was still trying to back away, her hands coming up defensively before her, when he reached her and lifted her from her feet, swinging her up into his arms. Holding her tightly against his chest, he carried her out into the hallway, heading for the stairs.

'Zarek, put me down!' Penny wriggled nervously in his hold.

'Keep still,' he warned as he mounted the stairs, ignoring her protests. 'And, no, I won't let you down—not until you see.'

'See what?'

He looked down at her for a moment. A searching, burning stare that seemed to flay away a much-needed protective layer of her skin.

'Until I make you see just how wrong you are.'

CHAPTER FOURTEEN

JUST how wrong?

That sounded shockingly hopeful.

Was it possible that there was something Zarek could show her, tell her, that could make this all right? In spite of herself, Penny couldn't subdue the tiny spark that suddenly lit up in her heart and made her feel so very different about the way he held her, made her stop fighting against his hold.

They were at the top of the stairs now, a couple of long strides across the landing and Zarek kicked open the door that led to their bedroom.

'In here.'

He carried her over to the bed and let her down onto the softness of the coverings. But then, when she would have jumped back up again, getting to her feet, not sure whether she needed to escape or should stay, he pushed her back into place, holding her still with the strength of just one hand. And looking up into his face, into the dark, barely focused eyes, the formidable set of his jaw, she suddenly had a rush of nervous panic.

Had she got this all wrong? Was Zarek not going to tell her what she most wanted to hear? Was his plan something else entirely?

Hadn't she played right into his hands by telling him that she'd lied about wanting a baby? Showing that she wanted to be with him, no matter what?

'Zarek—don't do this. Please.'

Tears burned the backs of her eyes. Tears of loss of the hope she had allowed herself to feel even if just for a moment. Tears of anguish and despair at the thought that he might once again be using only sex as a way of communicating with her. That still passionate desire might be all that he was feeling.

Tears of defeat at the thought that no matter how much she wanted to fight it, rationally at least, physically, she knew that she could not.

Defeat at the admission that she had settled for the sort of second best she had told herself she was never going to agree to. But she couldn't fight both Zarek and herself at the same time.

Even now just the touch of his hands on her sent excitement fizzing through her. Even now, the memory of being held close to the heat and hardness of his body as he had carried her up the stairs, the steel-hard strength of his arms supporting her, her head against his chest, made heat burn along the line of every nerve.

Even though his hands were now used to restrain her, keep her in place, she knew that she wanted them there, where they were holding her so tight that she couldn't move. Even though the powerful length of his denim-covered legs was so close to hers that she only had to move an inch or so to make them brush against each other. And his head was bent so that it was so close to her, his eyes boring into hers—but did they burn so intensely in an attempt to entice or to dominate?

'Zarek—let me go!'

She broke off as his grip tightened on her and he gave her imprisoned hand a tiny shake.

'Penny—listen. Listen—please.'

And it was that *please* and the voice in which he spoke it that stunned her, shocking her into silence and stillness, all the fight draining out of her in a rush.

'Please…' he repeated.

Suddenly it was as if the fighting had been all that had held her upright. Her spine sagged, her struggles stopped completely and she could only freeze into total stillness, staring up into the clouded darkness of his eyes.

'Zarek…' It was just a whisper. But his head was so close to hers that a whisper was all she needed. 'Just what are you doing?'

'Penny, don't fight—or talk—not yet. Just look at this…'

After that shaken, shattering *please* he'd recovered some of his self-assurance. The pleading note had gone from his voice but at the same time there was a strangely ragged sound to the words as if they—or he—were starting to fray at the edges.

He was turning her as he spoke. Practically lifting her bodily from the bed and twisting her round so that she was facing away from him and looking directly at the ornately carved wooden bed head. The one they'd been given as a traditional wedding gift and that she had seen for the very first time on their wedding night.

Recalling that night, the first night they had ever spent together, the night she had given him her virginity, Penny could only be grateful that she was sitting down. As it was she knew that her whole body was trembling in a way that Zarek, still holding her, must surely feel now.

He had been tender that night, careful and gentle as well as so ardently passionate that she had felt she were going up in flames just to be held by him, touched by him. Loved by him. At least at that time she had allowed herself to think of the word love, hope for love from him.

But that had been before Jason had warned her that the only thing that drove Zarek was the need for an heir. Hermione had commented on it too. And then she had seen it for herself, the determination to focus on the company almost to the exclusion of everything else. She hadn't realised then that Jason and his mother had their own personal agenda. In her naiveté she had listened to both of them and she hadn't turned to the one man who could tell her the truth.

But when she'd challenged him downstairs, he'd reinforced everything she'd feared.

'That's exactly why I married you,' he'd said. What else was there to say?

Swallowing hard, she looked up at Zarek's dark, intent face.

'Tell me about it,' she said, and she knew that she didn't just mean the carving on the headboard. The carving that danced before her eyes when she tried to focus on it.

But to her total shock and consternation Zarek suddenly shook his dark head. His mood seemed to have changed abruptly as he raked both his hands through his black hair, ruffling it in a way that was disturbingly appealing. The gesture took his hands away from her arms, releasing her completely, but Penny found that, although she was now free, the last thing she wanted to do was to escape. Now she was the one holding herself completely still, sitting on the edge of the bed, waiting, needing to hear what he had to say.

'I'm sorry,' he said, making her blink in shock as he dropped down beside her on the bed, sitting close but not too close. Somehow he managed to hold his long body away from hers so that he was not touching her, but at the same time she couldn't feel that he was holding himself away from her because he wanted to put distance between them. On the contrary, she had the impression that he was doing it for her sake. Because he didn't want to crowd her. Because he wanted *her* to feel separate from him until…

Until what?

'I'm going about this all wrong,' Zarek said suddenly. He was leaning forward with his arms resting on his thighs, hands clasped, staring down at the floor as if carefully considering what he had to say. 'I should have started with saying how sorry I am…'

'You just did,' Penny put in, but her response was greeted with another shake of his dark head.

'No—not for that—and that was not enough. What I mean is that I am so sorry for never understanding the reality of love.'

'I…'

Penny tried to speak but nothing would come. Had he just said *love*? And what did he mean?

'I'll admit that I never learned much about love. My mother was dead by the time I was four, and my father lost interest in life as a result. That was what left him open to Hermione and her scheming. When he became ill, I promised him I would make sure I had an heir—a member of our family to leave the company to.'

'So that was why you were so angry when you thought I was selling out to Jason. Not because you believed I had moved on to him.'

Zarek's eyes lifted briefly, burned into hers.

'You thought I was dead. You believed you were a widow. I couldn't expect you to wait for ever.'

'Oh, but…'

He hadn't heard her interjection, Penny realised. He was focused so intently on what he had to say that he talked straight through it.

'But you didn't, did you? I should have realised it from the start but it was only when I found those plans—the ones for the *Calypso*. I knew there was something wrong there but…'

'Zarek…'

She didn't know if he heard her this time, only knew that he turned to look at her, to stare deep into her eyes as if to draw the truth out of them. But at the same time what she saw in the black depths of his own gaze was that he knew the truth already. Knew it at a heart-deep, soul-deep level that needed no further explanation, no details. But he gave them anyway.

'One of the earliest plans was just right—perfect. It was everything I'd talked about, everything I wanted on that boat. But that was the one that was pushed to the back, kept at the bottom of the pile. And every other week there was a new one—one where you'd erased things, changed things, worked on the details a little more—when they didn't need it. And why…'

'I…' Penny began before she realised that he wasn't asking her why, but starting to tell her. That he had worked it out for himself and he really did understand. And because of that she knew she wanted to tell him herself. To let him hear the words from her mouth.

'I did it for you. I wanted to finish the designs on the *Calypso* because I knew how much it meant to you. I wanted the boat to be—to be…'

Remembered emotion made her stumble over the words.

'To be your memorial. But I knew that if it was finished, if *Calypso* ever went on sale, then I would really have to admit that you were gone and were never coming back. And I couldn't do that. And then Hermione—Jason—started pushing for—for a "rationalization" of the situation as far as Odysseus Shipping was concerned. But I said that I couldn't possibly think of that, not until I'd completed my memorial to you.'

'So you kept saying that it needed something new—something more. And you were erasing everything you'd worked on, showing them the incomplete version when all the time you had the perfect design hidden at the bottom of my desk drawer. You were holding them off, refusing to give in, in just the way that you kept all my clothes, when any sort of sense would say—'

'I couldn't let you go!' Penny cut in, needing to say it, to declare at least part of the truth about how she had felt even if she didn't dare to go the whole way. 'I just couldn't.'

'I know.'

There was such certainty in his tone that it made her stomach twist into tight, yearning knots. He had come so far but not quite far enough.

'I recognised what you were doing because it was how I was with my father. When I came home the only way I could win my father's attention was by being part of Odysseus Shipping—working for it—working with him. If I'd needed any proof that you'd loved me, it was there in front of me.'

'If…' Penny could only echo the word, unable to believe he'd actually used it. Had he really not needed proof?

'I realised that I was looking for "love" in all the wrong places. I saw it in the big things—like passion and hunger. I didn't know how to express myself any other way. I thought that if I gave you that you would know that I cared. And so when you started to withdraw from me I saw that as evidence that you had never loved me. Especially when you seemed to want to make sure that we never had a child.'

'The heir you wanted so much.'

'No.' Once more Zarek was shaking his head.

'No?'

'The child I wanted—or, rather, the child I didn't know I wanted until you made me so aware of the difference.'

'But you said…' Pain twisted in her heart, blurred her eyes as she remembered how he had stood before her and, calm, controlled, and totally certain, had declared, 'Yes, that's exactly why I married you.'

'I know what I said. And I had to say it because you asked for the truth. You insisted on it—and I wanted to be honest too. So I told you what it had been like. What had been in my mind in the moment that I asked you to marry me. I wanted you—*Thee mou* but I wanted you—and we both wanted a child. I thought that would be enough. It would make a great partnership. It was only later that I realised it didn't make a marriage.'

'When…?' She couldn't get the words out, the tears were so thick and heavy in her throat, almost choking her.

'When did I realise?' Zarek finished for her. 'As soon as I'd walked out on you in a rage. When I realised I was so damn furious because I was disappointed. On the *Troy* when I woke alone and missed you curled up next to me. On the pirates' boat when I thought that this might be the end—that I'd never see you again. In the black night on a black sea, when it seemed there was just one reason to hang on, to keep my head above water. I vowed that if I got out of there I would come back and tell you how I felt and ask you to start again. And this time I'd look for the smaller things, the quieter things. The things you gave when you worked on the *Calypso*—or last night when you came to my room.'

He paused, looked deep into her eyes as if searching for something and Penny could only hope that he found it in her own gaze because, even though her heart was so full of hope that she feared it might burst, she didn't dare yet actually speak what was in her thoughts.

'Just when I'd begun to realise how much brighter my life

was married to you, Fate took a hand,' Zarek continued. 'I was rescued—my life was saved but I lost my memory. I spent two long years wondering who I was—and wondering just why I always had this sense that something was missing. Something important. Something vital.'

'And when you came back…' He'd heard her saying she wanted him declared dead. Wanted to move on. 'That day at the beach…'

'I was totally off balance after seeing you with Jason. I had never known such a rage of jealousy before. Never cared enough to. But with you…'

Penny's breath caught in her throat like a small, uncontrolled sob that she couldn't hold back. She didn't know if Zarek heard it but his hands closed over hers, holding tightly but without that constraining quality they had had before. This time his touch was so much more gentle—she might almost say a lover's touch.

'It felt like I'd been given my life back only to have it—or the most important part of it—snatched away again just when I'd begun to realise how much it meant to me. I didn't know whether I'd been right all along and you were something so special I could never let you go. Or whether you had in fact been only concerned about Odysseus Shipping and all that it brought.'

His laugh was sharp, harshly ironic.

'Just when I'd realised how little the company mattered, I feared it was all that you wanted.'

'What I want…what I want is just you and me. Together. A man and a woman. Just as it was last night—'

She couldn't finish the sentence because Zarek suddenly leaned forward and stopped the words with his mouth, kissing them back down her throat. Penny stilled in shock, but not the fearful sense of being bewildered of just moments before. This was different. And it was close to something wonderful.

'I think now perhaps is the time,' he whispered against her mouth, his forehead resting against hers, dark eyes looking down into her blue ones. 'Perhaps now you could look at the carving. And before you say any more about the fact that I chose a mouse to represent you.'

Gently, with both hands on either side of her face, he turned her towards the bed head. The first thing that she noticed was that his hold on her wasn't quite steady. Something was making him shake, sending a fine tremor running down his arms, into his fingers in a way that told her just how important this was to him.

And this time her eyes were clear and focused. This time she could see what he wanted her to see.

A mouse, yes. But a mouse that was sitting upright, hanging onto something in its paw. And it was nibbling hard...

'What is that?'

'Rope.' His answer was soft but sure.

'Rope? Why rope?'

Zarek came closer, laid his head against hers, his cheek resting on her hair.

'Remember the story—a fable by Aesop where the lion let the mouse go and didn't eat her. Then one day the lion was trapped by hunters, caught in a net and the mouse came and gnawed through the ropes that held him, setting him free.'

'I remember.'

It was all that Penny could manage. Her mind was whirling with thoughts—wonderful, amazing thoughts.

'I was the lion and you were the mouse. You set me free.'

You set me free. Penny's heart jolted just once, hard and sharp against her ribs.

'But you weren't trapped.'

She spoke still with her eyes on that carving, not daring to turn, to look into his face for fear that this might all be a dream. That she might have it all wrong and he was not telling her what she thought he was saying.

'Oh, yes, I was. I was locked into a world I didn't want to live in. A world where only work and Odysseus Shipping mattered. Where I was prepared to marry solely to have an heir. A world where there was no love…'

Slowly, carefully, he turned her head until she was looking into his face. He kissed her once, softly, gently, heartbreakingly briefly.

'Not until you. After I met you. I couldn't get you out of my mind. I knew that I wanted no one else.'

'But you were so cool—so—'

'And you were so young,' Zarek told her, pressing a finger against her lips to cut off her anxious words. 'I was afraid that if I showed you the full force of my hunger for you—the way I really felt—I would frighten you too much, scare you off. But I wasn't prepared to wait. I wanted you as soon as I could have you. I had no suspicion then that fate had other plans. Plans that meant we would lose two years just when we needed them most.'

The way his eyes burned into hers told her of his answer even before he spoke.

'I should have told you before I sailed on the *Troy*, but we had rowed so badly. I was afraid. Things had been so difficult between us and I felt that if I told you, you would never believe me.'

'You might have been right.'

It was just a whisper of admission, her face sobering as she remembered how she had felt back then.

'I was feeling lost and unloved, totally unsure of my place in your life.'

'You didn't just hold the central place in my life—you *were* my life—my love—my heart. I thought that I would be back so soon that you would barely miss me. That then I could start again and show you just what you meant to me. I thought that we would have time to grow into our marriage. Instead of which—'

'No!'

Reaching up, Penny laid her fingers across his mouth to silence him.

'No more. It's time to put that all behind us. That was the past. We have the whole future to look forward to.'

'A future in which I can love you as you deserve to be loved.'

'And I can love you as a woman—a woman who loves her man. I'm not afraid or unsure any more. I've grown up. I thought I loved you when I married but it was as nothing compared to what I feel for you now. I want to be your wife and go into this wonderful future we can have together.'

She barely got the words out before Zarek had captured her mouth in a long, deeply passionate kiss. But it was also a kiss of love, of caring. A kiss that came from his heart, from the depths of his soul. And as he kissed her his hands stroked over her body, caressing, tantalising, arousing until she moaned for sheer joy of the feeling.

'And to prove that,' he whispered thickly against her mouth, holding her so close that she could not be unaware of the force of his need, his hunger for her. But this time it was a hunger that she knew was created by the passion of true love. 'Will you let me make love to you as the woman I love? The love of my heart, my life. My wife.'

'Willingly, *glike mou*,' Penny said happily, gathering him close in her arms and falling back against the pillows as she felt his warm, welcome, beloved weight come over her, his kisses on her cheek. 'I can think of nothing I'd want more—because I really believe that it's more than time I welcomed my husband home properly at last.'

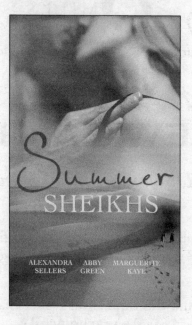

WEB/M&B/RTL2

Discover Pure Reading Pleasure with

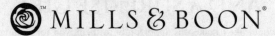

**Visit the Mills & Boon website for all
the latest in romance**

- **Buy** all the latest releases, backlist and eBooks

- **Find out** more about our authors and their books

- **Join** our community and chat to authors and other readers

- **Free** online reads from your favourite authors

- **Win** with our fantastic online competitions

- **Sign** up for our free monthly eNewsletter

- **Tell us** what you think by signing up to our reader panel

- **Rate** and review books with our star system

www.millsandboon.co.uk

 Follow us at twitter.com/millsandboonuk

Become a fan at facebook.com/romancehq

2 FREE BOOKS
AND A SURPRISE GIFT

We would like to take this opportunity to thank you for reading this Mills & Boon® book by offering you the chance to take TWO more specially selected books from the Modern™ series absolutely FREE! We're also making this offer to introduce you to the benefits of the Mills & Boon® Book Club™—

- **FREE home delivery**
- **FREE gifts and competitions**
- **FREE monthly Newsletter**
- **Exclusive Mills & Boon Book Club offers**
- **Books available before they're in the shops**

Accepting these FREE books and gift places you under no obligation to buy, you may cancel at any time, even after receiving your free books. Simply complete your details below and return the entire page to the address below. You don't even need a stamp!

YES Please send me 2 free Modern books and a surprise gift. I understand that unless you hear from me, I will receive 4 superb new books every month for just £3.19 each, postage and packing free. I am under no obligation to purchase any books and may cancel my subscription at any time. The free books and gift will be mine to keep in any case.

Ms/Mrs/Miss/Mr _____ Initials _____

Surname _____

Address _____

_____ Postcode _____

E-mail _____

Send this whole page to: Mills & Boon Book Club, Free Book Offer, FREEPOST NAT 10298, Richmond, TW9 1BR